Roy and Kay

Love in Litton – Legacy Series

Roy and Kay

THE BEGINNING

Lisa Smelter

Tampa, Florida

Roy and Kay: The Beginning

Published by Gatekeeper Press
7853 Gunn Hwy, Suite 209
Tampa, FL 33626
www.GatekeeperPress.com

The editorial work for this book is entirely the product of the author. Gatekeeper Press did not participate in and is not responsible for any aspect of this element.

Copyright for the images: iStockphoto.com/PeopleImages (young man), CoffeeAndMilk (young woman), TimAbramowitz (porch swing)

Library of Congress Control Number: 2022951475

ISBN (hardcover): 9781662922176
ISBN (paperback): 9781662922183
eISBN: 9781662922190

One

Roy heard from his mom that Kayleen Harris was back in Litton. She had been going to school at a big university in Illinois for the past four years. His mom knew about Roy's colossal crush on her during his junior and senior years in high school.

Kayleen was a strikingly lovely girl with long shiny black hair, beautiful bright blue eyes, an exquisite nose, a pale pink and white complexion, and a soft pink mouth. She had one of those soft and romantic-looking faces—like a black-haired Grace Kelly. She was tall and slender and moved gracefully, like a dancer.

Roy was tall in his teen years—five foot eleven inches—and Kayleen was just an inch shorter than he had been. During college, Roy grew even taller and now was six feet, four inches tall. Initially concerned about her height, Kayleen only dated boys who were taller than herself.

Kayleen and Roy shared some classes for the last two years at Litton High School. Since 'Harris' preceded 'Hillman' in the class seating plans, she usually sat either right in front of him or at least in the same row.

Roy remembered how her long shiny waist-length hair would sometimes fall onto his desk when she sat back in her seat. He used to gently brush it aside, but sometimes he just let it lay on his desk like a deep dark silken river. She used to wear a light flowery perfume, which he could still remember if he thought about it hard enough.

Kay, as she liked to be called, was a kind and friendly free-spirited girl. She was bright and articulate and often academically gave Roy a run for his money. It was acknowledged that Roy was the smartest boy in their class, but Kay was competitive and tried to outscore him on assignments and tests if she could.

Roy frequently grinned to himself when Kay turned around and challenged him. She always said it with a grin and was good-natured when he eventually received the higher score. Of course, there were a few times when she achieved a better score than he did, and she gently teased him about it. He just shyly grinned and accepted it with good grace. No one was surprised when he was the class valedictorian, and she was the salutatorian.

Because Roy had been such a quiet and shy boy, Kay never showed any romantical interest in him. Being hugely popular, Kay was asked out by the most popular boys and jocks. She didn't want to get serious with any high school boy, so she only casually went out with a few different boys. Her plan was to go away to college, so she did not want to be tied down with a steady boyfriend while she was attending it.

Roy remembered the first time he saw her. Her parents had moved her to Litton during her junior year. Her grandmother had a stroke and needed someone to live in her house and assist her with things she could no longer do on her own. Kay's father moved his wife and daughter from Illinois to Minnesota in order to care for his mother in her final years.

When Roy's homeroom teacher learned that Kay would be joining the class, he rearranged his seating chart. He liked his class to sit alphabetically, so half of the class moved back a seat to accommodate Kayleen Harris. Her seat was directly in front of Roy's that semester.

Just before she sat down that first day, she looked at Roy and flashed him a bright friendly smile with her perfect teeth. Roy felt his heart race and smiled shyly back at her. He had always been ashamed of his smile back then. He had a few crooked bottom front teeth. The dentist wanted Roy's teeth to stop growing before he corrected them. As a result, Roy didn't smile much, or if he had to, he smiled only slightly, keeping his mouth closed.

Because of her outgoing personality, Kay quickly made friends. She was nice to everyone, and, as a result, had many close friends. Once she found out that Roy was smart and liked challenging classes, she asked him all kinds of questions about their assignments. Kay was a curious girl, and Roy liked that.

Teachers enjoyed having both Roy and Kay in their classes because they were challenged by the duo to be their best. Either Roy or Kay would start interesting discussions in their literature or science classes. The rest of the class would roll their eyes when Kay and Roy started asking questions. As a result, Roy took all advanced classes his senior year. The students in those classes didn't mind his challenging questions.

Roy's father asked him why he had to take so many difficult classes. Roy told him that it was because he liked to learn about new things. His dad just wanted Roy to get through high school and be around to help him with the farm. It was then that Roy had to tell his parents that he didn't want to go into farming. He wanted a different career.

Roy's father reluctantly accepted the idea that his very bright and talented middle son was destined for another career that was not farming. Luckily, Roy's older and younger brothers were happy to follow their father's footsteps and work on the eighty-acre farm. They grew soybeans, sweetcorn, and peas, with a large apple orchard bordering the vegetable fields.

Roy's older brother, Tom Jr., was disqualified from military service because of his severe exercise-induced asthma. Thomas Sr. also had it. They walked around with their life-saving inhalers in their shirt pockets. They both had a few scary moments when they couldn't breathe, and their inhalers were on a bench or table somewhere out of reach. Mrs. Hillman finally got to the point where she had an extra inhaler for each of them in several rooms in the house as well as the barn.

Roy registered for the Vietnam draft and was quite willing to go and fight for his country if he was called up. However, he went right into college after graduation, and the draft passed him by. He watched his classmates go off to war and expected that he may have to go, too. The Hillmans were a patriotic family, and Roy was proud of his friends and classmates who did their duty by going to war when they received their draft notice.

Roy was an inquisitive young man who was interested in so many things. He loved to read literature and poetry. No one knew that he had the heart of a poet. Because he was a farm kid, most students assumed that he would be a farmer one day. He was interested in being a scientist or a writer, but his father convinced him that he should have a career that was more stable.

Because Roy was very good at math, his dad urged him to be an accountant. Roy was a good son and respectful, so he agreed to take up accounting in college. He could always do those other things in his free time, so he took as many tough math classes as he could at Litton High School.

Roy then went off to college to get his business degree in accounting. He started college early, taking summer courses. Young Mr. Hillman did not give himself a break while transitioning from high school to college life. He was just so anxious to get started on his college courses. Since he took a strenuous college load and had few distractions, he finished his four-year course in three years. That is why, at the age of twenty-two and a half, he already had a year of employment under his belt.

Kay was also good at math. She wanted to become a Registered Nurse. As a result of their intended careers, Roy and Kay typically had one or two classes together each day. They would see each other briefly in their twenty-minute homeroom and then in one of the advanced math classes that Litton High School offered. They seemed to end up in many of the same Language Arts classes, as well.

Roy remembered helping her with some knotty math problems a few times. She would turn around and sweetly ask him for some help. Their teachers liked the students to help each other, so they never got in trouble for talking in class. Little did Kay suspect that Roy's heart was in danger of leaping from his chest each time he spoke to her.

Roy held cherished thoughts and memories of Kayleen Harris for years. He didn't think that they would ever date. She was sweet and kind and friendly, but she was definitely "out of his league." He was a nice-looking boy, even though he was so tall and thin.

He went out for the track team and liked to run the long-distance marathons. Because he practiced running whenever he could, he was quite fast. First and second-place trophies in track resided on a shelf in his bedroom to prove it.

His quiet nature made him seem like a loner. He went out a few times with some nice girls, but he could never get past his crush on Kay. As a result, he grew up to be a reserved and quiet young man.

Roy's thin frame filled out in college. He conscientiously worked out with weights to build up his upper and lower body. Those knobby knees that looked out from under his track shorts in high school finally became regular, normal-looking knees. In fact, he now had very nice-looking long legs—not that he ever showed them off. He didn't even own a pair of track shorts anymore. At twenty-two and a half, he was now a tall, lean, but muscular, young man.

His thick dark brown hair, nice blue eyes, and handsome face, along with his fit physique, were very attractive to some of Litton's young female population. He had no conceit; in fact, he didn't even realize that some of his co-workers and neighbors drooled over him and wanted to get to know him better.

Roy was quietly brilliant at his job, but he really came out of his shell when he performed in the amateur play productions sponsored by the Litton Community Playhouse. Locals simply referred to it as the Playhouse. He was a very good actor and was much sought after by the directors of the various plays. If there was not an acting part that he was interested in, he would help build and paint the sets. The local neighborhood acting community loved Roy. He found a lot of happiness there. Roy didn't date much or go to many sporting events, but he did truly enjoy his time with the members of the acting community.

Well-read, Roy was able to talk knowledgeably about a large variety of subjects. He was a very kind, considerate, and respectful young man. Despite disagreements when they were teenagers, he now got along very well with his two brothers, and he loved his hard-working parents. Even though he had chosen not to go into farming, he often spent his weekends at his parents' farm, helping his brothers and father with the crops.

Roy helped his father with the business end of the farm, too. His dad regularly took Roy's advice when it came to buying or selling something regarding the farm. Thomas Sr. was so proud of Roy's career and good steady job. Farming was sometimes a gamble. There were many lean years tucked into the profitable ones. It all depended on the weather, and Minnesota was known to have its share of dry summers.

Situated in the oldest part of Litton, Roy's apartment was old and quite shabby. It was the least expensive one he could find. He didn't mind what the rest of the place looked like; what mattered was having a roof over his head. He wanted to live on his own, and he also planned to save as much money as possible. His long-term plan was to buy his first house when he was twenty-six. He didn't spend much money on entertainment because he rarely dined out or went on dates.

His mom taught him how to make economical nutritious meals. He took his lunch to work every day. As a result, his bank account was slowly, but steadily, rising. Roy had an old car that he kept in perfect condition. Working on his car was something that he enjoyed very much. He befriended a young mechanic who lived in his apartment building, and the two of them often worked for free on the cars of the older residents.

No one in those apartments had much money, and they all helped each other. Roy didn't advertise his good steady job, but he did a few nice things for his neighbors without them knowing about it. Broken lights in the hallway would suddenly be fixed, residents would find envelopes with a bit of cash inside in their mailboxes, and someone kept putting stacks of quarters on the communal coin-operated washers and dryers. Roy knew that he very likely had more money than his neighbors, and he found little ways to help them out. All the same, he was able to start saving quite a lot of his salary.

After work one fine Friday evening in June, Roy decided to stop for a bite to eat in the little cafe near his apartment. The Star Cafe was a mom-and-pop restaurant that served the best pizza burgers that Roy had ever tasted. It was one of his favorite foods, along with apple pie. He treated himself occasionally to supper after a long week at work. His family had been going to the Star Cafe since he was a small boy.

The owners were good friends of his parents. They were always happy to see Roy when he came in. He nearly always came in by himself and sat at the old-fashioned counter to eat. He was quietly friendly with the waitress and the owners. After a quick meal, he invariably left a nice tip for his hard-working waitress and drove home to his apartment. There, he would put on some music or read until bedtime. On Saturday mornings, he usually drove to his parents' farm and spent the day with them.

His weekend routine was a quiet one, but he was satisfied with it. During the week-day evenings, he usually spent some time at the Playhouse rehearsing for a play or just hanging around chatting with the people who were like-minded.

As he was finishing his simple meal, the bell on the door pinged, as it always did when a customer came in. He looked idly up and toward the door. His heart started to race when he saw the two young women who came in. Kay Harris was one of those women. Every one of his old feelings for her rushed back the instant he saw her again.

Kay was every bit as lovely as she had been at her high school graduation party. That was the last time he had seen her. Her long waist-length hair was now much shorter; it was still very shiny, but now it only came halfway down her back. Because it was a fine warm day, she was wearing a pretty, blue sundress. Her creamy shoulders showed under the straps of her sundress. She hadn't aged much in the four years since he had last seen her. She was smiling with that pretty, pink mouth of hers, and her eyes were sparkling with happiness.

As if she could feel Roy's intent gaze on her, she looked over and saw him. It was obvious from her look that she didn't recognize him for a few seconds. Then her eyes got wide, and an astonished look came over her face. As she got nearer, she smiled broadly at him.

"Hi. You're Roy Hillman, right? Do you remember me?" she asked in her friendly voice.

Roy nodded and smiled at her. It was the first time that he had ever given her his full smile. He had finally gotten his teeth fixed when he was in college. He endured braces for a year and a half. Now he had a very nice white smile.

"Hi, Kay. Of course, I remember you. It's only been four years since I last saw you. My mom mentioned to me a few days ago that you were back in Litton," Roy replied, barely containing his excitement at seeing her again.

He gestured that they should sit down next to him, but she smilingly shook her head and said, "Thanks, Roy, but I promised my friend, Martie, that we would sit in one of the booths and have a pizza burger. They're the absolute best here, don't you think?"

He nodded and smiled sweetly at her. Kay took her friend's arm and led her to the back of the restaurant. Roy watched them go and sit in the back booth. The wooden benches were carved with the initials of half of the students from Litton High School. There were hundreds of initials carved there. He had never carved his own initials because, somehow, he thought that it was vandalism.

Roy heard Kay laugh when she located her own initials and showed them to her friend. He didn't want to intrude, so he stayed seated at the counter and finished his beverage. As he sat there, he wondered if he should walk back there and say goodbye.

Kay called out, "Roy, if you have time, come back and sit with us, okay? I'd like to find out what you're doing now."

Roy was happy that she asked him to spend a little time with them. He smiled at his waitress, paid his bill, and handed her a three-dollar tip. That was quite generous for his small bill, but he knew that she worked hard and needed the extra money. She and her husband had a clutch of small children to raise.

Roy walked to the back booth. He was still wearing the blue suit that he had worn to work. The pale blue cotton shirt that he wore under the dark, navy blue suit and tie complimented his nice cornflower blue eyes.

People looked at him now and saw a handsome and successful young man. Roy didn't know that he exuded calmness and authority. His respectful job and success as an actor gave him a confidence that he didn't have in high school.

Kay slid over in her seat and indicated that he should sit next to her. He slid his long, tall body into the cramped booth. That was one of the reasons he always sat at the counter; there was more room for his long legs. Kay sat quite close to him. He could smell her flowery perfume.

First, he smiled nicely at Martie, and then he turned in his seat to look at Kay. Her eyes were bright, and she was smiling. *She is more beautiful than ever*, thought Roy, as he tried to quiet his pounding heart. He couldn't believe that he was sitting next to Kay Harris and that she had asked him to sit there. It was like one of his dreams came to life.

He smiled at her and lightly asked, "Are you home for good, Kay? Did you finish your nursing course?"

Kay looked carefully at him. She was so surprised at how good-looking he had become since high school. Why had she never noticed that before? Her memories of Roy were of a nice, hard-working, very smart, skinny boy who liked to challenge his teachers and herself with life's tough questions.

She couldn't believe how attracted to him she suddenly felt. His smile for her was warm and friendly. Since he had never smiled much at her in high school, it was a surprise to find that it did something to her. She got little butterflies in her stomach when he smiled at her like that. His nearness also affected her. He smelled great, like fresh pine woods. It must have been his after-shave.

She looked up at his face and smiled back. "Yes, I graduated a week or two ago with my degree in nursing. I had been living with my uncle's family while I was in college. They invited me to stay for a while longer, but my parents wanted me to come back to Litton. It's been a long time since I visited them. Also, my Nana is not doing very well. She is weak and very frail. I'm quite worried about her. I wanted to come home and spend some quality time with her. My dad wants me to take the summer off before I look for a nursing job. How about you, did you ever get that accounting degree? You certainly look like a businessman to me."

Roy responded quickly, "Oh, yes, I got my degree. Since I finished it in three years, I've been working for a year already. I am the accountant for the big new grocery store on Main Street. They're very good to me. I like it."

Kay curiously asked, "Do you still live on the farm, or do you have an apartment in town?"

"I moved into my own apartment during college. I love my parents and the farm, but it was too difficult to study and do my assignments while I was living there." He didn't mention where his apartment was located. While he didn't think that Kay was a snob, he didn't necessarily want her to know that he was living in the shabbiest apartment building in all of Litton.

Kay introduced Roy to Martie. She told him that Martie was a good friend from college. Martie lived in Chicago and had just completed her nursing degree at the same time as Kay. They were the best of friends. Martie was in Litton for a week while Kay showed her the sights. They were both unwinding from the intense last several weeks of finishing their nursing programs. Kay had been to Martie's home in Glencoe several times over the past four years, so it was time to reciprocate and show Martie everything that Litton had to offer.

Kay watched Martie's face as she talked with Roy. It was obvious to her that Martie was a bit enamored with him. Roy was friendly but didn't even register the fact that Martie was interested in him.

They talked for another half hour while the girls ate their food. When they were finished, he walked them out to Kay's car. She had a brand new sparkling white 1974 Pontiac GTO with red and blue racing stripes. Roy almost drooled over it. It was exactly the car that he would have chosen for himself if he was looking to buy a new car.

He commented on its beauty. "I love your new car. It's so clean and white. I could see myself in a car like that someday."

Kay smiled and said, "Yes, I love it, too. It was my college graduation present from my parents. They asked me what I wanted, and when we got back from the graduation ceremony, it was sitting in front of my uncle's house with a big red bow on it. I know that I am so lucky to have such great parents. They have given me so much." Her face was tender when she thought of her wonderful parents.

Roy thought back to a year ago to his own college graduation ceremony. His parents and two brothers had been there. His parents gave him a fifty-dollar savings bond. Roy was grateful for it. He was not envious; Kay deserved all the good things that came her way.

Kay was a lovely and kind young woman. People probably liked to give her things. She seemed to be a gracious receiver of gifts. Roy was always surprised that for a very lovely girl, who seemed to have everything going for her, including wealthy parents, she was so nice and generous. Kay never gloated over her possessions or flaunted them in front of people.

Roy remembered her graduation party. It had been at her grandmother's house, where she was living. Besides the gifts that she received, there was a big pile of colorfully wrapped gifts, all the same size. She gave all the graduates who came to her party a gift when they walked into the backyard. Roy still had that black "Class of 1970" photo album. At the party, her mom said that it was Kay's idea, and she had paid for all of them with her own money.

Roy put all his high school pictures in it. It sat on his shelf in his bedroom with his track trophies. He put Kay's graduation picture in it, as well as a few dozen of his other classmates. Of course, he did not look at their pictures as often as he had looked at Kay's picture that first year after she left Litton.

Now he hardly ever looked at it. What was the use—Kay was not going to be in his life in the future. It had taken him two years after high school to stop thinking about Kay so much. At one point, he just decided that he had to move on. Kay Harris, and his huge crush on her, belonged in the past. He had his whole life ahead of him.

He occasionally still looked through his senior yearbook, especially if he met an old classmate in town. Then he would walk down memory lane. He re-read his autograph pages and looked at the pictures of his classmates.

Because he and Kay sat next to each other in their homeroom class, they knew each other a little better than he knew some of his other classmates. They had exchanged yearbooks so that the other could write a few words of wisdom in there. Kay's words to him were, **"Roy, be strong and courageous."**

Roy knew that those beautiful words came from Joshua 1:9. It was a Bible verse that he had internalized as a young boy that always brought him peace and hope. It was uncanny that she had written those words. He didn't know if Kay knew the entire verse or its origins, or if she just thought they were words that kids said to each other in a yearbook. He was ready to give her the benefit of the doubt.

Roy remembered then that he wrote a few of Mother Teresa's quotes in her yearbook. He had wanted to say something profound but decided to write some uplifting words, instead. He said, **"Yesterday is gone. Tomorrow has not yet come. We have only today. Let us begin. Every time you smile at someone, it is an action of love, a gift to that person, a beautiful thing."** Roy hoped when he wrote it that she would read between the lines and understand that he thought that her smile was truly beautiful. But maybe she hadn't even really looked at his inscription.

Now she was back in town. He supposed that he would run into her from time to time if she stayed in Litton. He would probably be invited to her wedding and baby showers, in time. Those would be tough days for him.

Roy smiled at her and Martie. He shook Martie's hand in a friendly way and went to do the same for Kay. Only Kay was quicker than he was. She grabbed him and gave him the best hug of his life. Her arms squeezed his waist as if she had really missed him. Then, with a beautiful pink blush on her face, she let him go and stepped back.

Her eyes met his, and she said quietly, "It was nice seeing you and talking with you, Roy. I'm sure that I will see you in town one of these days. Have fun at your job." With one last smile, she opened her car door and got in. Martie looked at him once more with a wide grin and got in beside Kay. They shot away before Roy had a chance to get into his own car and go home.

Instead of reading that night, he put on some of his favorite music and remembered everything he could about Kay. As he sang along to James Taylor's version of "You've Got a Friend", he wished that he could say those heartfelt words to her. He would be there for her if she ever wanted or needed him. However, she didn't even know that he wanted to be her friend. He wondered if they could become friends, now that she was back in town. All he knew was that it was going to be difficult to forget that wonderful hug and the feel of her slender arms around his waist.

Martie wanted to talk about Roy later that evening in Kay's bedroom. Since Kay had a large full-sized bed, there was more than enough room for Martie to sleep there, too. Kay offered her one of the spare bedrooms, but Martie said it would be more fun to sleep in the same room so they could talk before going to sleep.

"So, Kay, you have never mentioned Roy in all the years that I have known you. Didn't you like him when you guys were in school together? I don't know about you, but I think he's a hunk! I certainly would have remembered someone like him." Martie came straight to the point. That was one thing that Kay really liked about Martie. She spoke her mind whenever she wanted to. While she was upfront with people, she was never unkind.

"To tell the truth, Roy didn't look like that in high school. He was always nice looking, but he was quite skinny, and he never smiled. He was always so intense and quiet. I think that college and his job must have been good for him. I must admit that he is now a very attractive man. So yes, dear Martie, I did notice him, too." Kay was just as direct as Martie had been.

"Do you like him? You have the first claim to him, but if you don't want him, you can give him to me," Martie said with an impish grin.

"Well, Martie, he's not mine to give. If he is interested in you, I say 'go for it'. Only how will we get to meet up with him again? Besides working at the new grocery store, I have no idea where he lives or what he does in his spare time. For all I know he already has a girlfriend, or he could be engaged or even married. Let's ask my mom in the morning what she knows about him. She has lots of friends in Litton. She might have heard something." Kay spoke forthrightly.

The two friends finally talked about other things and then drifted off to sleep. The next morning Kay asked her mom about Roy. Anna Harris was quite surprised. Kay had never shown any preference for Roy's company in the past.

Anna was one of the Playhouse enthusiasts and saw Roy quite a bit. She thought that he was a very pleasant and respectful young man. They had been in a few productions together. She admired his dedication to the plays and his helpfulness to all the cast.

"Well, honey, Roy Hillman is a budding young actor. He usually participates in the plays that we put on through the Playhouse. I usually see him there once or twice a week. I'm sure that he's not married or engaged. I think that I would have heard about it if he was. He has never brought anyone with him to the Playhouse. When did you run into him?" Anna didn't want to seem too curious, so she spoke very matter-of-factly to her daughter.

Kay told her about their unexpected meeting with Roy at the Star Cafe yesterday. She said that she and Martie enjoyed talking with him and wanted to see him again before Martie went back to Chicago.

Anna looked at Kay with her raised eyebrows. Was it Martie who wanted to see Roy again, or was it Kay? She would love it if Kay got involved with someone nice like Roy. Then she might marry and settle down in Litton. Kay had been talking recently about looking for a nursing job in a bigger city and moving away. She was a bit unsettled after graduating from college.

Anna was pretty sure that Roy planned to settle down in Litton. His friends and family were all here. If Kay fell in love with him, she would be more likely to stay in Litton. That would make Anna and her husband, Sterling, very happy.

"Oh, I didn't know that Roy liked to act, although I'm not surprised. In high school, he really got into the plays and literature that we read. He was always asking questions about the plots and characters. When are you going to the Playhouse again, Mom?

Do you think that Martie and I could come with you?" Kay asked hopefully.

Anna told her that she would be going to the Playhouse on Monday evening. The director would be looking over a few plays to decide which one to put on next. The usual actors and actresses quite often showed up to put their two cents worth into the discussion. Anna told Kay that she was sure that no one would mind if she and Martie tagged along. It was quite often a loose and casual gathering, with an open invitation to everyone who was interested in volunteering at the Playhouse.

Kay and Martie agreed to go with her to the Playhouse on Monday. That left them today and tomorrow to do other things. They planned their weekend carefully so that Martie would get to see all that Litton had to offer. Since the weather was beautiful, they planned to do a lot of things outdoors. Martie didn't plan to drive back to Chicago until next week on Thursday.

CHAPTER

Two

Roy drove to his parents' farm on Saturday morning because he wanted to get involved with something that would take his mind off Kay Harris. He thought about her non-stop all last night. She hadn't mentioned wanting to see him again, so he probably wouldn't run into her for months or maybe never if she moved away again. He was so preoccupied that his mom asked him what was wrong, but he just shook his head slowly and told her that there was something that he needed to think about. Roy led her to believe that it was about his job. She didn't press him to talk about it.

The whole family sat down to a simple Saturday lunch. Roy loved his mom's homemade apple butter. She always made some in the fall after their apples were harvested. She sparingly gave him a jar of it every few months during the year. He had a new jar opened and in his fridge at home. Now he spread some lavishly on his piece of homemade bread. With a slab of butter and a swish of apple butter, it was almost the best thing he could think of to eat.

His mom chuckled and said, "I don't know why you are still so thin, Roy. Whenever you come over, you eat half a loaf of my homemade bread with that apple butter. Where do you put it?"

Roy laughed. "I have long hollow legs, Mom. Your bread helps to fill them up. I look forward to coming here every Saturday and eating this delicious food. Why do you think I come over so often?" He nudged his brother, Tom. "It certainly isn't to see Tom's ugly mug."

The two brothers good-naturedly elbowed each other and traded insults until their mom told them to stop that and eat their lunch. Thomas Sr. ignored their antics and concentrated on eating his food. He only said something to his wife and boys when they irritated him beyond his tolerance level. As a result, he rarely said anything at all, unless it concerned the farm.

It was the same every week and had been since Roy was a boy. Tom and he had been sworn enemies when they were younger. Tom was two years older than Roy and was always bossing him around. For a quiet boy, Roy had not tolerated it. He gave back, verbally, every bit as much as he received from Tom.

It had been Tom who made Roy dislike his own name. Royal was a family name. It was his mother's maiden name. She and her husband had named their boys Thomas Junior, Royal, and John. Tommy, as he had been known back then, used to give Roy a sharp thump on the back and taunt him with the phrase, "You're a Royal pain in the butt." He never said it in front of their parents, though.

Roy was a nice boy, and he never told his parents, but he hated to be called Royal. He had insisted from the time that he was ten years old that he wanted to be called Roy. Tommy continued to call him Royal on the sly until Roy moved out to go to college. While Roy was in college, the two brothers made up their differences and now were quite good friends.

They both gently teased their younger brother, Johnny. He was a very quiet stocky teenager who never said a word to anyone. He worked hard on the farm, doing whatever his dad told him to do. No one ever knew what he was thinking. Johnny was intelligent and got good grades in school, but he was more of a loner than Roy had ever been. No one in their family knew him very well.

Roy tried to talk with Johnny to see if he was doing something that bothered him, but Johnny curtly said, "No", and that he was fine. He just didn't want to talk about anything. Roy made him promise to come to him if he needed anything. Johnny reluctantly agreed. That had been a few years ago. His family still didn't know how to treat Johnny. Johnny was almost six years younger than Roy and still a mystery to him.

After lunch, Roy helped his mom with the dishes. None of the others even thought of doing that. Once the meals were over, their father took Tom and Johnny back outside to work for a while in the big sheds. There was always something to do for the farm. Thomas had long ago decided to let Roy hang out and talk with his mother after lunch.

Selma told her husband that she wanted to visit with Roy and find out what was new with him. Over the years she showed Roy how to make many meals and how to take care of his household. She taught him how to do his laundry, clean the house, cook the meals, and make a grocery list before shopping.

If he shopped without a list, he was bound to get all the wrong kinds of groceries. He would buy too many products that were impulse buys, and he would forget the staple ingredients that he needed on a weekly basis. Roy now followed her advice. He had gone grocery shopping a few times without his list and was astonished to find that she was right.

Selma Hillman was a practical and kind woman who loved her family. She never asked for anything or complained. She just trudged along, doing all the housework and cooking and raising the children. She knew that her husband loved her and wanted her to be happy. It was just that he didn't openly show it very much. Her sons, Tom and Johnny, were very like their father. While they appreciated her and all that she did for them, they forgot to let her know that.

Roy, looking in from the outside, could see all of this. He intentionally told her as often as he could that he loved and appreciated her. He also told her that the others did, too, even if they didn't say it very often. Selma thanked him for his sweet reassurances to her. She secretly admired Roy's defense of the other males in the family.

After they finished the dishes, they sat down at the kitchen table to talk. Selma spent most of her time there. Roy quietly told her that he recently ran into Kay Harris and her friend, Martie. He said that Kay looked as beautiful as ever and that they had talked for an hour at the Star Cafe. He told her about Kay's sparkling white new car. His mom could tell that he was not envious, just intrigued.

Selma listened carefully. She wondered how Roy felt about seeing Kay again. She didn't think that he had ever quite gotten over his massive crush on Kay. He certainly didn't take many girls out, and he never talked about his dating, if he did.

She knew that he met any number of women at his job and through the Playhouse. Recognizing that he was somewhat shy and reserved, he had nevertheless come out of his shell quite a bit since he graduated from college. Now he was finally talking about a girl, and wouldn't you know it, it was Kay Harris again.

Selma asked him about Martie, but Roy was not able to tell her much. To tell the truth, he had barely noticed Martie. He had been sitting next to Kay. Their thighs accidentally touched a few times when he maneuvered in the seat to get more comfortable. The legroom in those booths just didn't accommodate his long legs. Because of Kay's proximity, a herd of buffalos could have walked past him, and he wouldn't have even noticed them.

Selma always encouraged Roy to talk and share his thoughts and feelings. Because of her loving influence over the years, Roy was able to share his innermost thoughts. He doubted if she ever shared those revelations with his father. Dad didn't seem to want to know or talk about things like the plays and Roy's opinions regarding something or other.

Roy was grateful to his mom for prompting him to talk about the things that mattered to him. Someday, he wanted to be able to know how to share his thoughts and feelings with his wife. Unlike that of his parents, he wanted a more verbally intimate relationship. He knew that his mom longed to be able to talk with her husband. However, Thomas was always too busy or simply unable to really talk about their lives and family.

So, not having anyone else with whom to connect emotionally, Selma was grateful have Roy to talk to about her feelings. He was a good son. She looked at him with love. He turned into such a handsome young man. She really couldn't understand why he didn't go out with more girls. She heard through the usual grapevine that some of the young ladies in Litton thought that he was very cute and a good catch.

Roy quietly said that he hoped to see Kay again, but he wasn't sure when or how that would happen. Really, nothing had changed, even though she was back in Litton. Selma hoped that he would either get over his crush or ask her out. It would really be something if they found out that they were meant to be together.

Roy went outside and helped his father and brothers until supper time. After supper, he returned to his apartment. On Sundays, he liked to go to church in the morning, read the Sunday papers, and take himself for a long walk. He had been thinking for a long time about getting a dog. A dog would be fun and would provide company. The apartment building manager allowed residents to have dogs and cats, provided they were well-behaved.

After work on Monday, Roy went home, changed, ate a quick supper, and then drove to the Playhouse. He looked down at his nice-looking outfit. It was one that his mom had given him a few weeks ago. She had seen it at the store and thought that he would look good in it. It was a pair of tan khaki cargo shorts and a blue and white striped polo shirt. It was very fashionable, and Roy looked quite nice in it.

Outside of his professional wardrobe, Roy never cared very much about his own clothes. He usually just wore something that was comfortable, without regard to how nice it looked. His mom wanted him to start caring about what he looked like, so she told him to wear these new clothes when he went out into the community this summer.

He looked forward to seeing his friends and acquaintances at the Playhouse. The group was going to choose a new play tonight. He drove his old car into the parking lot. He parked right next to a new white Pontiac GTO. It looked just like Kay's new car. He wondered which one of his friends had gotten a new car. He admired its style and white sparkling perfection before going into the building.

He went up to the stage where people were already sitting. As he looked around, he saw Kay and Martie sitting with Anna Harris. He was a little surprised to see them. He knew that Anna Harris was Kay's mother. In their two-year association as Playhouse actors, she never once mentioned Kay's name. He respected her privacy and never asked about Kay, either. He smiled cheerfully at all of them and took the nearest available chair.

Kay and Martie turned to look at Roy and smiled at him. Both ladies simultaneously thought the same thing. *What a hunk Roy is! I wish that he would come over and talk with me.*

The director came in, and they started to discuss the possible plays. Kay and Martie were introduced, and everyone nodded a silent greeting. It was usual for the group to have extra people there. People came and went in this business.

Roy tried not to look at Kay too often. He was very aware of her, though. She looked extremely pretty in her short blue jean shorts and pink halter top. Her long legs and slender arms and shoulders were uncovered, and it gave Roy a jumpy feeling. He was not used to seeing so much of her lovely body exposed.

After the group decided to put on the play, *Our Town*, the director took note of all the usual actors and actresses seeking roles. He had some questions about which teenagers could play the parts of George and Emily. Most of the volunteers were adults. A few of them had teenage children whom they might be able to coerce into trying out for those roles.

During the discussion, the director walked up to Kay and Martie. He thought that Kay looked perfect for the role of Emily, except that she was about five or six years older than Emily was at the beginning of the play. He asked her if she was interested in volunteering for the play.

Kay, who had always liked the theater, agreed to read the play again and decide which part she might like. The director had already decided that Roy would be perfect either as the Stage Manager or George as an adult. It would be difficult for the audience to see six-foot-four Roy as sixteen-year-old George, as he was in Act 1 of the play.

Anna Harris stated that she was interested in playing either Mrs. Webb or Mrs. Gibbs, the mothers of Emily and George. Since Kay looked so much like her mother, the director thought that Anna would be perfect as Mrs. Webb, with Kay playing her daughter, Emily.

Martie led Kay to where Roy was sitting talking to the director. She put her hand on Roy's arm and asked him, "Are you going to volunteer for this play, Roy? If you are, will you let me know when the play will be shown to the public? I might be able to drive over from Chicago to see it. It would be nice to see some people that I know in a play. I would be too afraid to act in one myself, but I certainly would be willing to pay to see the performance." Her voice was soft and beguiling.

Kay had to hold back a laugh. Martie acted in quite a few plays in high school. Kay saw pictures of her acting in them when she visited Martie's home. Martie had the type of personality that was perfect for acting, even professionally. *Now what is Martie up to?* Kay wondered with an inner grin.

Roy looked at the hand on his arm and quietly smiled at her. "I think that I might try for one or two parts in the play. Do you know the story of *Our Town,* Martie?"

"Oh, we read it in high school. I think that I remember what it is all about. George and Emily are in love and get married, right? And the Stage Manager narrates the whole story. Do you want to play one of those parts?" Martie wanted to know.

"Yes, either one of those parts, I think," Roy said slowly. He turned to look at Kay, who was standing silently next to him. "Are you going to try out for one of the parts, Kay? I seem to remember that you were in the One-Act Play in high school. Do you still like to act?" he asked her quietly.

"Yes, if I decide to stay in Litton, I will try out for one of the parts. It doesn't have to be a big role. After all, I am a newcomer. So many of the other women have volunteered for a long time. My mom told me that she has known most of the actors who are here tonight for several years," Kay said quietly. She usually had a lot more to say. For some odd reason, she felt shy hanging around Roy. This was not like her normal bright and outgoing personality.

It was still quite early, only 7:45 pm. Roy decided to ask Anna and the girls if they wanted to get a cool beverage somewhere. He turned to Anna and asked, "Anna, do you and the girls want to go to the Dairy Queen with me and get a beverage or a cone? It would be my treat. It seems a shame to go home so early on such a beautiful evening."

Anna smiled. Roy had never once asked any of the volunteers at the Playhouse to join him at the Dairy Queen. She usually saw him get into that old car of his and drive away, without having invited anyone to do anything. Was he asking now because of Kay or because of Martie? Her darling Kay was quite beautiful, but Martie was very pretty, too.

"I'm interested in going. How about you girls?" Anna asked Kay.

Kay and Martie quickly exchanged glances. Both smiled, simultaneously. "I'm up for that. How about you, Martie?" asked Kay.

Martie smiled widely and said, "Lead on, Macbeth."

Roy smiled at Martie's obvious pun about the Playhouse. He led the way to their cars. He watched Kay get into the driver's seat of her new car and usher Martie into the passenger's seat. There was no room for anyone else. Anna turned to get into her own gorgeous dove gray Bentley Corniche.

It was the most beautiful car that Roy had ever seen. How he wished that he could afford to buy one for his mom. She would feel like a million dollars in one of those lovely cars. Anna offered him a ride.

"Roy, would you like a ride in my car? I know where the Dairy Queen is. It's only a few blocks from here. We might as well go in one car."

Roy wanted to experience the ride in a car like that. It would be something to describe to his mom on Saturday. He agreed and sat back to enjoy the ride. Anna was a good driver. She treated the car like a lady, but not an old lady. He would like to see what this lovely car could do on the open road.

They had a marvelous time at the Dairy Queen. Roy saw a lot of people that he knew. They all looked surprised to see him with three lovely women. Kay and Martie were openly flirtatious with Roy. At first, he didn't know how to react, but then he just let himself go. It was surprisingly easy to gently flirt back at them. He even tried it with Anna, who laughed quite a bit. They all had so much fun that evening. It was unfortunate that it was getting late, and Roy had to be at work by 7:30 the next morning.

He reluctantly said goodbye to his beautiful companions when Anna dropped him off next to his car. Kay pulled up next to her mom's car to say goodbye to Roy. She looked at his car without any expression on her face. He hoped that she didn't pity him for having such an old car. It ran well, so he didn't have any plans to trade it in for a newer one.

They planned to meet back at the Playhouse on Wednesday evening to audition for their parts in the play. Martie wanted to come with Anna and Kay to see Roy one last time before she drove back to Chicago. Kay and Anna could tell that Martie was very attracted to Roy. It was a pity that she lived six hours away from him.

Martie talked about Roy all evening. Kay was just as enamored with Roy as Martie was, but she didn't want to compete with her friend. Roy had looked at her a few times and smiled right into her eyes. His eyes seem to say that he liked her. *Had he done the same thing to Martie?* Kay didn't know.

It was going to be a bit tricky for the next few days. They would be seeing Roy on Wednesday. Would Martie come right out and ask Roy how he felt about her? She was straightforward in her conversations with others. It was refreshing for her friends and a bit disarming for strangers. At least they knew where they stood with her.

As outgoing as Kay usually was, she could not see herself asking Roy if he liked her. That would make her very uncomfortable. She would rather have a sign from Roy telling her that he liked her. That was the way it usually happened. Boys and young men usually told her that they liked her before they asked her to go out with them.

Roy was so different. Maybe he would not do that, but then how would she know if he liked her? She wished that she could be alone to just think quietly about Roy. She had very seldom liked anyone as much as she liked this new image of Roy.

Tuesday was spent helping Kay's Nana with the garden. Kay's grandmother adored summer flowers. Long ago, she planted a bunch of beautiful flowers all along the edge of the house, from front to back. They were beautiful, and their scent was heavenly. She especially loved the old-fashioned big fragrant cabbage garden roses. Her flower beds also held a lovely assortment of dahlias, peonies, and camellias.

Kay inherited her grandmother's love of flowers. She could spend hours outside with her grandmother, just weeding and tending the flowers. They talked together about all kinds of things while they worked. It was one of Kay's favorite things to do with her Nana. Kay planned to have flowers growing around her home when she got married. She knew everything about how to grow them and care for them.

Martie didn't care for the garden work so much, so she went inside after thirty minutes. She would rather help Anna with the cooking. Anna was an inspired cook who liked to make up her own recipes. That intrigued Martie, who had a strong creative streak. Her own parents had a terrific housekeeper who kept the family wondering what new creation she would think up for their supper each evening. Martie loved the variety of food that she was offered at home.

Kay was very close to her grandmother. She was always surprised at Nana's good advice. It was almost as if she understood Kay's generation very well. Mrs. Harris only had two sons. She missed not having a daughter with whom she could teach things that were important. While she liked her daughter-in-law, Anna, it was Kay who she really loved. She had given Kay the benefit of her wisdom ever since Kay and her parents moved in six years ago. While her son and daughter-in-law brought Kay up to be a kind and considerate young woman, it was her grandmother's advice that Kay really took to heart.

"Remember Kayleen, beauty is fine when you're young, but it doesn't last. Kindness and charm will be yours your whole life. They are much more important than beauty." Nana tried to get Kay to see that beauty wasn't everything. It made Kay into a girl without much conceit.

Another of Nana's gems was, "Never flaunt the possessions you have, girl. Not everyone was as blessed as you were to grow up in a family with money. Having more money than someone else NEVER makes you superior to them. Some of the most beloved people in the world had no money. Think of Mother Teresa. Now there was a much-loved woman. Money didn't mean a thing to her, other than as a means by which to help others. She gave away everything that she ever had. No, I say give generously of your money. Make others happy with your gifts to them. You don't need all of it. Oh, it's nice to have enough money, but don't let it be important to you. You would still be a darling girl even without a penny to your name. Remember that always, my girl." Nana's old voice was strident as she said that to Kay.

Now that Martie had gone inside, Kay decided to tell her Nana about Roy. She explained that they had just been casual friends in high school, but now that she had met him again, she was very attracted to him. When Nana asked why that was a problem, Kay explained that Martie was also very interested in Roy. She didn't want to have to compete with her best friend.

Nana wisely counseled Kay to just be herself. If Roy was attracted to either of them, it should be for him to choose between them. "Let him do the chasing," she counseled Kay. "Men like that anyway. They don't want to be caught; they like to do the catching."

Kay said that she could understand that. Roy seemed to be a very traditional type of man. He would probably like to do his own chasing and catching. He might not be interested in either Martie or herself. He might already love some other girl.

After a heart-to-heart talk that evening, Kay told Martie that she was not going to pursue Roy. Although she was attracted to him, she would just be friendly toward him and let him make his own choice. If he liked Martie, she would be happy for her friend. If he cared for someone else, Kay would still enjoy being friends with him.

Martie agreed. She wasn't sure if she would speak up and tell him that she liked him or not. She had no problem telling someone that she was attracted to them. She was surprised by, and pleased with, Roy's gentle flirting on Monday. She sensed that it was something that he didn't do often. That made her think that he was more than a little interested in either Kay or herself. If he preferred Kay, she could handle that. Kay was a dear person, and very beautiful. She, herself, was just pretty, in her own eyes. Still, she couldn't predict what type of person Roy was more attracted to.

As she thought about it some more, Martie thought that maybe she would be the lucky one this time. Over the last four years, she had witnessed many young men fall for Kay's beautiful and feminine looks. While Kay was unfailingly polite, she never reciprocated their feelings. As much as she loved and admired her friend, Martie sometimes felt a little frustrated that Kay was the one who was most often sought out by the young men they met.

A long-distance relationship with Roy could be difficult, Martie thought, getting ahead of herself. Maybe she should think of moving to Litton. She was sure that there would be some nursing jobs open around here. Her new life was just beginning. Why not embrace it with open arms? After all, you were only young once. Funnily enough, that was exactly what Nana had told Kay yesterday.

After work on Tuesday, Roy took himself shopping. He couldn't wear the same summer outfit again tomorrow. His old clothes were not fit to be seen anymore. He wanted to have three or four comfortable, but stylish, new sets of summer clothes.

Roy called his mom and told her that he wore the clothes she gave him and really liked them. He asked her where she bought them. His mom chuckled and said that it was about time that he started caring about his wardrobe. She told him where to go to find similar outfits. As she hung up, she wondered if he wanted to look nice for Kay. He hadn't mentioned her, but she knew him well and could tell that he wanted to impress someone.

Roy found three more nice pairs of cotton cargo shorts in a variety of colors and four more polo shirts. He figured that he could mix and match the shirts and the shorts. The friendly salesclerk flirted with him and showed him shirts that complimented his hair and eyes.

He found that gentle flirting was fun. *Why haven't I ever tried it before?* he asked himself. It created all kinds of interesting options for Roy. He had found it so difficult to talk to young women before. Now, with just a clever comment or two, couched in a flirtatious voice, he had no trouble at all talking to a pretty girl.

He was surprised when the salesgirl, Alicia, gave him a slip of paper with her name and phone number on it. She said that she would go out with him if he called her. Roy nodded and put the piece of paper in his billfold and promised to think about it. If things didn't work out with Martie or Kay, he might give Alicia a call. It was time for him to spread his wings and start dating a bit more. While his heart wanted it to be with Kay, he had to be realistic. She had never shown that she preferred his company. He received more feedback from Martie and Alicia than he ever had from Kay Harris.

Kay's Pontiac and Anna's Bentley were already in the Playhouse parking lot when Roy got there on Wednesday. He parked in the spot nearest to them and looked down at himself. His dark gray cargo shorts and yellow and teal green polo shirt looked pretty good. He hoped that Kay would like them, too.

He decided to audition for the part of George Gibbs. He hoped that Kay would try out for the part of Emily Webb. That would make them a couple in the play. George and Emily fell in love in high school and married three years later. Roy would certainly enjoy working on the script with Kay. They would have quite a few scenes together.

The stage was full of people. Roy saw Anna, Kay, and Martie standing near the director. Roy walked up to them to say hello. He saw a warm welcome in the eyes of all three ladies. Having acted with Anna a few times previously, he thought that she was a lovely and kind woman. It was no wonder that her daughter was so incredible. Anna chatted with Roy for a few minutes about other actors.

Martie and Kay listened quietly until they were done talking. Then Martie lightly patted his arm and said, "Good luck on your audition tonight, Roy. I'm sure that you'll get whatever part you want. If you don't mind, I'd like to talk with you for a couple of minutes after the tryouts, okay? I promise that I'll be quick." She smiled nicely at him.

Roy nodded and returned her smile. If he wasn't still crazy about Kay Harris, he might have been attracted to Martie. Her interest in him was obvious. It was easy to like her pretty face and warm personality.

He turned to look at Kay. She was quiet again tonight. She looked very lovely in an old-fashioned blue and white dress. It looked like one that the character of Emily would have worn in the 1930s. She probably wore it on purpose to get into character. He hoped again that she was going to try out for the role of Emily.

Roy prepared well for the role of George. His portrayal was superb, and the director gave him a big thumbs up when he was finished with his script. Roy sat back and observed the other auditions. He thought that Anna made a good Mrs. Webb and Mrs. Gibbs. Kay tried out for the role of Emily. There were two other young women vying for that role, as well.

Although he would have preferred to work with Kay, he thought that one of the other women was equally good. Her name was Letty, and he had worked with her on previous productions. Roy thought that the director might go with Letty because she was a good actress, and he was familiar with her capabilities.

All the auditions were done by eight o'clock, and the director dismissed them. He said that he wanted a day or two to make his decisions, but he would be there on Friday night to announce the cast. If the person he chose was not there on Friday night, he would call them at home on Saturday morning.

Roy walked Anna, Kay, and Martie to their cars. He had not yet had that quick talk with Martie. He offered to take her home to Kay's house after their talk. Martie looked excited about that and agreed. She looked at Kay with raised eyebrows and told her that she would be home in half an hour or so. Kay nodded, smiled, and waved to them when she drove away.

Roy ushered Martie into the passenger's side of his old car. Martie said that she didn't want to talk in the car. She asked him if he knew of a place where they could talk uninterrupted.

Roy drove to the college campus, which was only a few miles away. There was a great little gazebo that was usually open during the summer. There were bench seats all around the inside of the gazebo. He sat there many times during his college days when he wanted a quiet place to study.

People tended to forget about it when school was not in session. Roy drove past it a few times on his way somewhere and noticed that it was usually empty. He walked her into the vacant gazebo and sat her down on the wooden bench.

Martie looked at him with admiration in her eyes. She decided to tell Roy that she was attracted to him. She was leaving tomorrow, so there would be no harm done if he was not interested in her.

"Thanks for allowing me to talk to you, Roy. I'm driving back to Chicago tomorrow and wouldn't have any other chance. I'm a bit nervous, but that's okay, right?" Martie looked at Roy intently.

Roy took one of her hands in his and quietly said, "Go ahead, Martie. I'm listening,"

Martie looked at their linked hands and smiled. "I know that I've just met you, Roy, but I am really attracted to you. I wanted to know if you were attracted to me, too. I would definitely go out with you if you asked me. You probably think that I'm pretty forward for saying all of this, but that is the way I am. I tell things like I see them. I don't like to waste time."

Roy wondered what to say to her. He decided to tell her the truth— or at least part of the truth. He was not interested in dating her, but he liked her as a friend.

"First of all, thank you, Martie. I'm flattered by your interest in me, but I need to tell you that I really like someone else. It's a girl that I met before I met you. Things are complicated, and we are not dating yet, although I am hopeful that we can start dating sometime this summer. I would really enjoy having you as a friend, though. I would be happy to write to you or talk with you on the telephone. Do you think that you want to be my friend? I admire you and think that we have some things in common. What do you think, Martie?"

Martie looked downcast for just a moment, but then she smiled wryly. "It figures—you're too cute and nice to be free from attachments. Yes, I would like to be friends with you. I'll give you my address and telephone number in Glencoe. That's the suburb in Chicago where my parents live. Until I know where I will move to, you can write to me there. I hope that you will write or call me and tell me when your play will be shown to the public. I'll ask Kay if I can stay with her for a day or so. I'd love to see how everything worked out. By the way, I thought that your portrayal of George was really inspiring. You're a good actor."

They talked for a few more minutes. As they stood up, Roy bent over and gently kissed Martie's cheek. She turned her head quickly and kissed him right on the lips. Roy hadn't kissed many girls and had never been kissed first by one of them. He enjoyed her quick kiss and pressed his lips back for just a second before he broke their kiss.

Roy smiled at her and walked her to his car. As he drove back to Kay's house, they chatted lightly about nothing much. Martie asked him to come inside and say hi to Kay and Anna. He declined, saying that he still had a few things to do tonight. He told her to have a safe trip back home. She blew him a kiss from the steps and waved to him as he drove away.

When Martie went inside the house, she told Kay and Anna about her talk with Roy. She looked at Kay with a sad face when she told her that Roy was interested in someone else. Kay felt sad, too. Her attraction to Roy would very likely come to nothing if he already liked someone else. Kay helped Martie pack her suitcase and put it in her car, in preparation for her early morning departure. They had a quiet, but very nice evening.

The next morning, after waving goodbye to Martie, Kay went to talk to her Nana. Kay told her what Roy told Martie. She was a little sad about not having the chance to get to know Roy better. He apparently liked someone else.

Her wise Nana said, "Well, I warned you that men liked to do their own chasing. I'm glad that you didn't tell Roy that you like him. Your plan was just to be friendly anyway, right? So, nothing has changed. Still, be as wonderfully warm and friendly as you can be. He will see you as you really are. Maybe he will come to like you more than that other girl. It sounded like there were complications in their relationship, anyway. You can't force someone to love you, you know. All you can do is be yourself. They will either come to love you or not. It is not up to you. I hope that you are not too disappointed, love. All I can say is that if you and Roy are meant to be together, you will be. Remember that."

Kay hugged her grandmother tightly. She was always comforted by Nana's words, even if her grandmother didn't sugarcoat things. Nana told the unvarnished truth, but she put a positive spin on most things. Her grandmother was right, if she and Roy were meant for each other, they would get together. If not, Kay hoped that she would find the man of her dreams. She knew as well as her Nana that you can't force someone to love you.

Roy thought about Martie's confession that she liked him. He felt bad about her, but he could not date her when he still could not get Kay's lovely face out of his mind. He liked everything about Kay. Besides her soft beauty, she was so nice and kind. She was smart and confident. She was interesting and competent. In fact, she was his ideal woman.

Unfortunately, Roy didn't know what Kay thought about him. He could only be himself around her. His hope was that she would get the role of Emily, and he would be able to play opposite her as George. *Well, I will know tomorrow,* he thought.

*   *   *

Friday evening, Roy wore yet another of his new outfits. His cargo shorts were black, and he teamed them with a cobalt blue polo shirt. He didn't know it, but the shirt made his eyes look deep blue. He had a good tan going from spending a lot of time outside on Saturdays at the farm.

Many of the women at the Playhouse gave him a second look when he walked up to the stage. They couldn't remember when Roy had ever looked better. He was such a handsome man. *Why is he unattached?* they all wondered.

Roy waved hello to Anna and Kay, who were sitting about five feet away from him. The director arrived with a flourish, using the opportunity to stage a dramatic entrance. He proclaimed the names of actors and actresses, along with their respective roles in the play. Even the understudies benefited from his good mood and flair, as he loudly bellowed their names to the rafters. It was all in fun, and even those who were disappointed to not receive a role relished their part in his mini extemporaneous production about the casting of this play. Amid this revelry, Roy found out that he would be playing George in Acts 2 and 3 when he was older and married to Emily. A dark-haired teenage boy would be George in Act 1.

A pretty, teenage girl was given the part as young Emily in Act 1. Letty would be playing Emily in Acts 2 and 3. Roy smiled at her. He thought that she was a good actress. They never had any trouble working with each other before. Kay was asked to be Letty's understudy. She quietly nodded and accepted her role. Anna was given the role of Mrs. Webb, Emily's mother. Anna's big grin was fun to see.

Only after all the parts were announced, did the director present a serious tone as he shared the rehearsal schedule. He gave everyone a copy and told them that he would see them next week. The understudies were to come to rehearsals as often as they could. They could miss a few times, but it was important that they understood everything that was going on with the play.

As Roy walked out with Anna and Kay, he smiled at them and asked them if they wanted to go someplace for a cool beverage. It was quite hot that night. Anna looked at Kay, who slowly shook her head no. Anna reluctantly declined the invitation and said that Roy should ask them again sometime.

Kay had been so quiet all evening, and now she apparently didn't want to hang out with Roy. *Something is up,* Anna thought. Roy nodded and smiled slightly at them before getting in his car and driving away. Kay got into her mom's car and sat silently all the way home.

Once inside their house, Anna turned toward her daughter and gently asked, "Kay, darling, what's wrong? You've been so quiet all evening. I'm surprised that you didn't accept Roy's offer to go somewhere after rehearsal tonight."

Kay avoided her mother's gaze lest she noticed the wetness in her anguished eyes.

"Oh, I guess that I am just a bit tired, you know." Then, attempting to change the topic quickly, "I'm so proud that you got the role of Mrs. Gibbs! You'll be wonderful."

Anna wasn't buying it. She persisted.

"Kay Harris. I'm your mother. I usually don't intrude, but I know when things are not right. Now, tell me. What is troubling you?"

"Mom, I don't want you to change how you are with Roy. I mean, you're castmates and friends. You've had the last two years to build a friendship as adults. I've been . . . away at school and, now that I'm back . . . I don't know." Kay's voice trailed off.

Anna gently hugged her daughter's shoulders and said, reassuringly, "It's okay, I understand. It can be hard to know how to act around someone you haven't seen in a while . . . and might be attracted to now . . . "

At that, Kay looked up to her mom and said, "Mom, I . . . " Then the tears started, and Kay rested her head on her mom's ready shoulder.

They stood like that for several minutes, mother consoling daughter, neither saying another word.

Then Kay collected herself.

"Mom, it's okay. Roy doesn't owe me an explanation. It's just that I find myself having feelings for him. I'm just as surprised by this as you possibly are. But I can't and won't do anything to get in the way of Roy and this girl he's apparently intending to date this summer."

Kay abruptly turned to make her way upstairs to her bedroom, then paused to add, "It's like Nana says, 'If we're meant to be together, then we will.' I know that."

Kay seemed neither convinced nor buoyed by Nana's words at the moment and instead resumed her sad sojourn up the stairway.

"Kay?" Anna called out.

Turning around at the landing, Kay faced her mother.

"Sweetheart, I don't know how Roy feels about you, but everyone else has always loved your wonderful personality. Please try to recapture that. Find your joy, again. Meanwhile, none of us knows how things may work out between Roy and the girl he apparently likes. Let Roy see you as you've always been."

Kay nodded and smiled at her mom.

"You're right, Mom. Goodnight." Anna blew her a kiss, and then they both went into their bedrooms.

As Roy drove home, he wondered why Kay had been so quiet all night. The Kay he knew had a fun personality and was outgoing. He hoped that she wasn't too disappointed that Letty had gotten the lead role. He would still get to see Kay, though. She was supposed to come to the rehearsals and learn Emily's lines in case she ever had to step in for Letty.

The next day he told his mom that he was cast in the role of George in the play. He told her that Kay was offered the role as understudy to Letty, who played opposite him. He briefly told her the story of *Our Town*. Selma nodded and looked thoughtful. Roy would be seeing quite a lot of Kay, then. She wondered how that would go.

Selma smiled when Roy told her about Martie and her kiss on him. He also told her about Alicia, the salesgirl at the store. Selma could see that Roy was attempting to break out of his reserved shell. She totally endorsed his plans to date more. He was wearing the outfit that she picked out for him. She saw how handsome he looked in it. He told her that he had bought a few more outfits that were like this one. Selma grinned even wider at that news.

Kay made a conscious effort to forget about pursuing a relationship with Roy. Her warm and fun personality returned like a spring flower. After meeting some old friends from high school on the weekend, she agreed to go out with an old boyfriend. She stressed to him that she was not looking to get serious with him. She only wanted to go out and find out what he was doing these days.

On Tuesday evening, everyone showed up for rehearsal. Roy was glad to see that Kay had regained her sweet and fun personality. Her upbeat and friendly smile for everyone sparked his curiosity and had him watching her surreptitiously. He managed to talk with her while the director was working with other members of the cast. He found himself smiling and even laughing about some of the things she said and did. She was all over the place, getting beverages for people and running errands for the director, who was pleased to find such a go-getter in her.

At the end of rehearsal, Roy wanted to ask Kay and Anna out for a cool beverage but didn't want to get shot down again. He quietly said goodnight at the door and got in his car and drove home.

Anna had been about to call after him to see if he wanted to join them, but Kay quietly told her that it was okay. They could ask him out next time. Anna was happy to see Kay being her old self tonight. The director smiled broadly at Kay's back when she rushed off to do some errand for him. Anna hoped that he would not take advantage of Kay's willingness to do things for the others. She had seen him do that with all the new people until they got tired of it and flatly refused.

CHAPTER

Three

The summer slowly passed. Roy continued to enjoy Kay's warm and wonderful personality at the rehearsals. He truly missed her when she was absent. One night, Anna told him that Kay had gone somewhere with an old boyfriend. It was true, and she wanted to see how he reacted to that news. She was not disappointed upon seeing how quiet he got when she told him about Kay and Steve.

Roy knew who Steve was, easily recalling him from high school days. Steve had been a popular football player in their class. Everyone in the school knew that Steve went out with Kay as often as she would agree to it. He never made a secret of his interest in her. *Steve is okay,* Roy thought. Only he acted kind of superior to a lot of the other guys in their class. Roy did not like that. He just hoped now that Steve was treating Kay right.

If Roy dated Kay, he would treat her like the lady that she was. He would give her anything that she wanted. *Oh, to have one date with the fair Kay! If she ever kissed me, I could die happy,* he thought wistfully.

Roy contacted Martie a few times during the summer, each time providing updates on the play. He had to tell her that he had still not resolved the conflict with the girl that he liked. She laughingly told him that he had better do something about that soon, or she was going to drive to Litton and claim him for herself. He laughed back and jokingly pleaded for some more time. She told him that she wanted to see this girl at the play on opening night and admonished him that he had until then to ask this girl out. Roy wondered how he could resolve his issue with Kay. It seemed as if she was dating Steve again. Anna had recently told him about another date that Kay had with him.

Roy didn't know what to do about his unresolved feelings for Kay. After spending so many nights rehearsing and talking with her, he now knew that he loved her with all his heart. It was no longer just a crush. There had never been anyone else in his life except Kay.

It was a struggle to stay friendly and upbeat with her at rehearsals. He just wanted to sweep her into his arms and give her a long lingering kiss. This was new for him. He had never thought about kissing so much in his life.

Kay continued to casually date Steve and a few other old friends. She cherished her nights at rehearsal so she could hang out with Roy. Her feelings for him had deepened, and she was now very aware of him and would have dated him exclusively if he had just asked her. Her Nana reminded her on a weekly basis to let Roy come to her if he was interested. She should be open and friendly with him and let him see that she enjoyed his company.

*   *   *

As the summer progressed, Kay's Nana became more fragile every week. She was too weak to go into her flower garden anymore. Kay made sure that Nana's windows were open so that she could see and smell her beloved flowers. Kay's parents were worried, too.

Her dad hugged Kay fiercely when he told her that he didn't think that his mother would be with them much longer.

It was a warm summer day in the middle of August. Kay sat next to her beloved Nana and held her hand. Old Mrs. Harris had hardly any breath left, and what she had was shallow. Kay had just told her that she finally realized that she was in love with Roy Hillman. Kay's Nana gently squeezed her hand with what strength she had left.

Her voice was so soft and shaky that Kay had to bend close to hear her. Nana quietly told her that in that case, Kay should show him, not in words, but in actions that she cared about him. Nana said sadly that she wished she would be there to see how it all turned out for her beloved Kayleen. Other than that, she was ready to be called home.

Nana was the only person that Kay ever allowed to call her Kayleen. It had been her Nana's mother's name. Nana's mother had died when she was only twelve, and she had missed her mom for the rest of her life. She wanted her mother's name to live on, so Nana convinced her son to name their baby girl that.

Kay thought it was such an old-fashioned name. It really didn't fit her personality. She was quick to tell all her teachers and professors that she wished to be called Kay. Kayleen was her real name, so it showed up on all her transcripts and any legal documents. It was on her driver's license. But her love for Nana allowed her to accept it when she called her that.

Kay knew that she owed her grandmother so much. She had welcomed Kay and her parents into her home for the last six years. She gave Kay everything that she needed, especially her wisdom and unconditional love. Kay was the person she was today because of Nana's love and care.

Kay went to look for her mom and dad. She could tell that Nana didn't have much time left. Her mom and dad gently hugged and kissed Nana goodbye. Kay sat with her in case Nana wanted to say anything else to her. Nana looked at Kay with such love and tenderness in her tired old eyes and softly said, "I love you, my girl." Then she closed her eyes and peacefully slipped away. Her passing was so quiet that Kay barely knew when it happened.

When she realized that Nana was gone. Kay brought her grandmother's thin frail hand to her lips and kissed it one last time. "Goodbye, Nana. I love you, too. I'll take care of your flowers for you." Kay's hot tears fell onto Nana's old frail hands.

It was a sad day for Kay to get through. She helped her mom and dad deal with the formalities and plan the funeral. She had been stockpiling pictures and mementos for the past several months, ever since she came home to Litton. She wanted to make a big poster board and display of memories in the house for Nana's friends to see when they came over after the funeral. She told her mom about her ideas, and Anna promised to help however she could.

Anna called the play's director and told him what had happened to Nana. He told her not to worry about rehearsals. They could work around Anna's parts. Her role was not one of the main characters, anyway. He said that Kay knew Emily's lines well enough and that she didn't need to come to rehearsals for a few days if she didn't feel up to it.

The Harris family got busy getting everything set for the funeral and the visitation at the church. They planned to host a light brunch for the neighbors and friends at Nana's house right after the funeral. Sterling and Anna really appreciated Kay's help with everything. Besides being such a lovely and sweet daughter, she was also level-headed and practical.

Even though he knew that his mother was fading fast, Sterling Harris was shocked by the grief he felt at her passing. He loved his mother very much. Anna was helpful to him, but it was Kay who helped him work through his grief. She spouted off words and advice that sounded exactly like his mother. Of course, that is where Kay got her wisdom. She soaked up all of Nana's words of wisdom for years, and they came back out just when they were most needed.

The sun was shining on the day of Nana's funeral. The funeral was set for 10:00 am. After the visitation and then the funeral mass, attendees walked to the old cemetery behind the church. Anna arranged for the church choir to sing Nana's favorite hymns. Having first led the congregation in song in church, the choir was now standing off to the side of the grave to sing one more song as Mrs. Harris' coffin was lowered into the ground.

Sterling and his brother, Roland, were standing next to the coffin. Anna, Kay, and Roland's wife, Ruth, and their son, were sitting in the uncomfortable chairs next to the grave. Kay was determinedly dry-eyed for the moment.

As she sat there, she thought about Roy for a minute. She was aware of, and appreciated, his presence at the funeral, noticing him seated at the very back of the church. She smiled shyly at him when she walked past him during the recessional. *How like Roy*, she thought, *to show his support as discreetly and modestly as possible.* She wondered if Roy had someone like Nana to give him sage advice. He certainly was every bit the gentleman. The very last piece of advice that Nana had given Kay was to allow Roy to see her love through her actions. She wasn't quite sure what that meant, but she would think about it some more.

Her thoughts meandered to the play rehearsals. There had been no sighting of Roy's mystery girl, nor did any word about her pop up in the usual gossip accompanying rehearsals. Kay wondered if he still liked her, whoever she was. Martie told Kay recently that Roy and his secret girl still hadn't resolved their issues. *Maybe,* she mused, *he would stop trying with her and be open to getting to know someone else.* Kay hoped with all her heart that Roy would turn his full interest toward herself.

After Nana was lowered into the ground, Kay and her extended family left the cemetery to drive home. The caterers were already there, setting up the food for the brunch. Kay spent the last day or so getting her grandmother's display ready. She tastefully arranged the pictures of her grandmother as a child, in school, getting married, family pictures with her husband and sons, various family gatherings, holding Kay and her cousin, and finally sitting down amongst her flowers in front of her house. That was Kay's favorite picture of her grandmother. That is how she remembered her.

Kay made a few beautiful displays of her grandmother's flowers, too. The whole living room smelled like Nana's cabbage roses. The display was a labor of love from Kay, and it was beautifully done. Kay thought that her Nana would be looking down at it and giving her a big thumb's up.

The house was full of people in no time. It was up to Kay to keep people moving around and not standing in the doorway. Because of this, she saw and spoke to everyone who came in. There were only two or three people that she didn't know. Because of her friendly personality, she soon discovered who they were and passed them on to her father or uncle.

She was standing in the doorway talking to one of her mom's friends when she saw Roy walk up the steps. He had two small bouquets of summer flowers in his hands. His eyes were dark and somber when he walked in. His small smile for Kay lit up his blue eyes. He looked very tenderly at Kay. He remembered how he had felt last year when his grandmother passed away. He came forward and handed her one of the bouquets and gently kissed her cheek.

"Hello, Kay. I'm sorry about your grandmother's passing. How are you holding up?" Roy asked quietly.

Kay was so happy to see him. She was thankful for his gentle kiss, as well. "Hello, Roy. It was so nice of you to come. I'm doing okay. Thank you for asking. How are you doing? I haven't been to rehearsals for a week. You'll soon be getting ready to put on the show for the public, right?"

"I'm doing well. Thanks for asking about me. Yes, the show is coming up quickly. We have all missed you and your mom at rehearsals. It's just not the same without your pretty face there." Roy didn't care if she was shocked by his words. She did have a pretty face, and he really did miss her.

Kay was surprised at Roy's choice of words. He had never said to her face that she was pretty. While she understood that she looked nice, she had never known that Roy thought that about her. That was good news for her to hear. She could use all the encouragement that she could get regarding Roy.

"Why, thank you, Roy. That's so sweet of you to say." Kay's face was flushed a pretty pink. With her shiny black hair, blue eyes, and lacy black dress, the pink flush made her look even more beautiful than usual.

She invited him in to say hello to her mom and dad. He told her that the other flower bouquet was for Anna. Since she had to stay near the door, she couldn't hang out with Roy. He talked with Sterling and Anna for ten minutes, had some of the food, and then left about half an hour after he had arrived. As he walked back out the door, he stopped to talk with Kay again.

"That display of your grandmother was very touching. Something tells me that you had something to do with it. Am I right?" Roy asked quietly.

Kay smiled widely at him. How observant of him. "Yes, that was my farewell gift to my Nana. I think that she would have liked it, too. Just before she died, I promised her that I would take care of her flowers. It was one of her great joys in this life. I wanted to show people how much she loved them. I guess I'll never be able to move away from here; I don't want to break my promise to her." Kay smiled at her little joke.

Roy very softly said, "I hope that you never move away. If you did, I would miss you very much." He just stood there looking at her with calm eyes as if he was daring her to say something back.

Kay's eyes widened and her flush came back—this time a deep pink. "Thank you, Roy. I think that is the nicest thing that you have ever said to me."

Roy was on a roll, now. "Do you think that I could come over and talk with you this evening after everyone has gone, and you're all feeling tired and flat from the day? I know how you feel. I went through the same thing last year when my grandmother died. It was a hard day for me, too. I just want to be here in case you feel like talking to someone about her. I never met your Nana, but I imagine that she was very like my grandmother. Would you like me to come back so you can talk to someone?"

"That is so nice of you, Roy. Yes, I think that I would like that very much. I'm not sure what my parents, uncle, and aunt have planned, but I'm sure that they will be okay if I get out of the house for a while to talk with you. How about 7:30 pm? Is that too late?" she asked anxiously. She didn't want Roy to retract his offer to come over.

"7:30 is perfect. I'll see you then, Kay. Until then, take care of yourself and your parents." Roy smiled a soft smile at her, waved his hand, and then went down the steps. Kay watched him walk to his car and get in.

She always marveled that his old car still worked. She wondered if Roy could not afford a newer car. Not that it mattered one bit to her. She would still love him even if he did not have one penny to his name. Her Nana had been right. Money was not that important in the long run. As long as you had enough to pay your bills, that was enough.

Four

That afternoon, after the guests had gone home and the caterers cleaned up the food and the mess, the Harris family went into Nana's study to hear her lawyer read the will. Sterling had made this room his office these last six years. He kept his Chicago business going through this office.

He made the trip to Chicago every two weeks to check on his business, though. It was a large accounting firm that served many Chicago Fortune 500 companies. He had hired a local Chicago manager to run his company after he had been forced to move to Litton six years ago to help take care of his mother.

His younger brother, Roland, was a doctor. It had been too difficult for him to move his wife and son to Litton. Sterling's job was much more mobile, so he volunteered to move his family, instead. He and Anna missed their old house and lifestyle in Chicago. They had been members of an exclusive local sports club. It was there that Kay had learned to swim and ride horses.

Horses were Anna's passion. She taught Kay everything there was to know about riding and caring for horses. They had their own horses, which were stabled a few miles away. Since Roland and his family were still in the Chicago area, they had temporarily taken over the horses for Sterling and Anna.

Anna very much missed seeing and riding her horse, Midnight. He was a striking jet-black Morgan. Anna talked to her sister-in-law every week, and she never failed to ask how Midnight was doing. Ruth and Roland made sure they took very good care of Midnight and Sterling's magnificent horse, King.

Anna made sure that she visited and rode Midnight whenever she got back to Chicago. Sterling drove to the Chicago area often, and sometimes Anna tagged along to visit with her old friends, see Ruth and Roland, and ride her beautiful Midnight. Sterling smilingly indulged Anna when she told him every month or two that she absolutely must go to Chicago to see her horse.

Kay's horse, Sunny, was small and gentle. Years ago, Sterling and Anna had purchased Sunny for their darling little twelve-year-old Kay. While Kay and her parents were back in Litton, they chose to loan Sunny to the private riding school near Roland's home so that young riders could learn how to handle a sweet-natured smaller horse. Kay loved Sunny when she was younger, but now as an adult, she thought that she would like a larger and more energetic horse. At almost five feet eleven inches tall, Kay was too tall for Sunny.

After Ruth told her how much the riding students adored Sunny, Kay told her parents that she would like to permanently donate Sunny to the riding school. They agreed with her. Sterling told Kay that he would buy her another horse, if she wanted one. Kay told him to hold off buying her one for now. She wanted to get a nursing job and see how much free time she had first. They agreed that it was a sensible idea.

There were a few places in Litton where they could go to rent a horse for the day. Kay rode a few horses from those rental places when she was in high school and had enjoyed herself. It would be easier to rent a horse when she had the time, rather than trying to ride her own horse every day while she was working full time as a nurse.

Kay had gone to several wonderful schools in Chicago. She took dance lessons from the time that she was four years old until she was fifteen. She dreamed of being a professional dancer until she grew too tall. When she topped five feet nine inches on her fifteenth birthday, her dance teacher gently told her that she was still growing and would likely grow to be even taller. Sterling was well over six feet tall. Tallness ran in the Harris family. Kay's teacher convinced Kay that she would be too tall to be a professional dancer. Male dancers would not be able to lift her and swing her around.

Kay had been quite upset about that, but the discipline and exercise had left her a tall, willowy, and very graceful girl. That was something that she was grateful for, at least. That was just about the time that she started to become interested in becoming a Registered Nurse. She always liked the idea of helping others heal and get well.

After she spent a good amount of time in a Chicago hospital visiting her dying maternal grandmother, she was convinced that she could be a good nurse. She had watched her grandmother's nurses carefully and thought that they did such an important job. She liked the idea of being useful and needed in her job.

Kay grew up with enough money to buy anything that she wanted. Her father and mother taught her that money was nice, but not something that she should ever brag about to anyone. That idea caused Kay to be a generous girl to her friends. She knew that nurses were not paid very well, but she was enthusiastic about going into nursing, anyway.

As they got comfortable in their chairs, Kay looked at her father and smiled warmly at him. Whatever Nana had done with her property was fine by Kay. She didn't want or expect anything in the will. She had several of her grandmother's favorite pieces of jewelry and a few other personal items. Kay was content with having those mementos of her beloved Nana.

Kay smiled at the thought of her marvelous life. Her parents were very generous, and she could make her own way once she got a nursing job. Of course, she hoped to marry one day, but she didn't expect her parents to help her out after she was married.

Everyone, except Sterling and Roland, was very surprised when they heard how much Nana's estate was worth. Since Roland and Sterling helped their mother draw up her will, they knew what was in it. The cash and the stocks were to be divided equally between her two sons.

Kay was astonished to hear that Nana had left her this house and all that was in it. Kay's cousin, Frederick, was given Nana's property in Northbrook, Illinois, which is where she grew up. It was currently being cared for by a distant cousin, who had been allowed to live there if she kept the property clean and up to date. That cousin would be given a nice chunk of money when she turned the property over to Frederick on his twenty-fourth birthday. This suited Frederick very well, since he was still in college and living in the Chicago area.

Kay loved this old house and its large yard and garden. *I will now be a woman with property,* she thought to herself. If she decided to stay in Litton, she would make this her home. Of course, it would be much too big for just herself. She hoped that her parents would want to stay with her until she either married or got a roommate. *I will be able to tend to Nana's flowers,* she thought happily.

It was an old house, built in the 1920s. It had five large bedrooms, as well as a formal dining room, two living room areas, a huge kitchen, a pantry, an office/study, and two bathrooms. There was a sturdy porch wrapped around the front of the house, with a dear old porch swing hanging in the corner. It was sheltered from the sun and rain, and the swing had a big soft cushion on it.

The swing was Kay's very favorite place in the whole house. She sat there many a night when she was working on her homework in high school. She sat on it with dates and with her Nana. It was pleasant to gently swing on it while sitting in the dark, smelling the roses and other flowers that were just around the corner from it.

Kay would see if Roy wanted to talk with her on the porch swing this evening. It wasn't very private, but she didn't suppose that he would need her to be in a private place. As far as she knew, they were just going to talk. It was secluded enough that a few of her dates in high school had snuck a kiss or two.

Kay smiled to herself at those memories. *Would Roy be tempted to sneak a kiss or two?* she wondered. She very much hoped for that, although he could just want to talk. Whatever he wanted to do, Kay was excited about seeing him and spending more time with him.

After the lawyer left, Kay sat talking with her dad and mom. Uncle Roland and his family left as soon as the will was read. He tenderly hugged her goodbye. They had gotten quite close in those four years that she lived with him, her aunt, and cousin while she was in college. She was good friends with Frederick and her Aunt Ruth, too.

It was nice to spend a few days with them before the funeral. Roland needed to get back to his medical practice. Frederick was longing to go back and see his new girlfriend, too. Aunt Ruth usually just went along with the crowd. She was always just happy to be with her family.

Kay and her parents talked about Nana and how she had been wise to leave the house to Kay. Sterling knew that Kay loved the old house. He wanted to find out if she would be okay if he and Anna moved back to the Chicago area. He had been keeping his business afloat for six years, but it was a difficult task. Kay talked with them about possibly getting a roommate or two. If she could manage that, she would be okay with her parents moving back to Chicago.

They talked about the possibility of Kay getting married. Kay blushed at that. She had not yet told them about her love for Roy. She only confided that important information to her Nana.

Anna had a pretty good idea that Kay was very attracted to Roy, though. It would solve all their problems if Kay got married and her husband moved into the house with her. That would be the only way that Sterling would really feel okay with moving out and going back to Chicago with Anna.

*　　*　　*

Kay dressed in a pretty, pale pink sundress for her talk with Roy. With all the time she spent outdoors in the yard, her skin was a luscious light brown. The pink dress showed her tan off to perfection. Her feet were a bit sore and uncomfortable from being confined in those new dress shoes for the funeral and brunch, so she decided to go barefoot. Her feet were narrow and dainty, and she painted her toenails a soft pink color to match her dress. She didn't know if Roy would notice them, but she liked the way they looked.

Kay told her parents that she was going outside to sit on the porch swing after supper. They nodded. It was the place where

Kay inevitably went when she wanted some alone time. They had plenty to do and talk about with each other anyway.

Sterling had seen a fabulous house in Northbrook last week when he was in the Chicago area doing business. The house was next door to an associate of his and was for sale. If they could just get Kay situated with a roommate, he and Anna could think of moving back to Illinois.

Roy drove up right on time. He looked searchingly at Kay for a minute without saying anything. She looked so sweet and beautiful in her pink dress. He looked for any sign of tears and was glad to see that she was dry-eyed. His smile was kind, and he immediately went over to the swing. She slid over and patted the cushion.

"Sit down here with me, please, Roy. This is the most comfortable seat in the house. The night air is so beautiful that I didn't want to go inside." She looked up at Roy with a sweet smile.

Roy sat down and turned to look at her. He didn't know if he should start talking or just let her talk. After two minutes of comfortable silence, he decided to start their talk.

"How are you feeling, Kay? Was today a trial for you, or did it make you feel better?" His voice was quiet and kind.

"I'm doing okay. Thanks for asking. I think that it was good for my parents, my uncle's family, and me to host that brunch today. It was wonderful to see and talk to so many of my Nana's friends. I know that I cried some of the time, but her death is still so recent. I know that she was ready to go; she told me so herself. It's those left behind who are the sad ones."

Roy nodded, knowingly. If she allowed it, he would tell her about his beloved grandmother who had passed away last year. She was right, it was the ones left behind who felt the hurt. He had no doubt that his grandmother was happy in heaven.

Kay talked for more than half an hour about the closeness that she and her Nana shared. She mentioned the words of wisdom that Nana gave her over the years. Her Nana had been a practical, loving, kind, and considerate woman. Mrs. Harris was proud of her two sons and their successes in life. She adored Kay and Frederick, too.

Because he lived in Chicago and was a boy, Nana didn't spend the same amount of time with Frederick as she had with Kay. She was still proud of the nice young man that he had become. He always sent her such nice cards for her birthday, Christmas, and Grandmother's Day.

Kay was her Nana's special little love, though. Her natural friendliness and outgoing personality had been a delight to her grandmother. Kay knew that she pleased her Nana, right up to her death. While she talked about her Nana, Kay's pain eased and became bearable. Her face was tender when she talked about her grandmother to Roy.

Roy felt very good being there for Kay. He knew that she needed to talk to someone about her grief. He was there for his mom last year, too. Selma had been devastated by the passing of her mother. While they hadn't talked much in later years, Selma still deeply loved her mother.

It was Roy who spent the most time in the last ten years with Martha Royal. She was a gentle woman, who had all kinds of unfulfilled dreams left inside her that she had never shared with her husband or two children. Roy shared his love of poetry with his grandmother. He was her favorite grandson. Martha's son, Stanley, went into the Army right out of high school and never married.

Of Selma's three sons, the only one who understood Martha's dreams was Roy. He was the only grandchild who inherited the Royal physique. They tended to be very tall and lean. He and Martha shared a kindred spirit. She told him that many times.

Her most prized possession was a very old book of poetry that she, in turn, had inherited from her grandmother. It was an original hardcover copy of Elizabeth Barrett Browning's *Sonnets from the Portuguese.* Her favorite poem, like so many others, was Sonnet 43.

Roy had memorized it by the time he was sixteen. He loved those beautiful eloquent words. Before she died, she laid her precious book in his hands and told him that she wanted him to have it. No one else would treasure it as he would.

Roy accepted it with gladness and promised to keep it safe. Roy knew that the book was very valuable, but he would never sell it unless he needed a lot of money in an emergency. It was sitting on the shelf in his bedroom which held all the things that were precious to him.

While they talked, Roy gently took Kay's hand and held it. She didn't mind a bit. She was just happy to have him there tonight. *He is being so sweet to me,* she thought.

As the evening stretched toward night, the gentle breeze played with Kay's long hair. She had left it loose, and now she had to brush it back from her face because the wind kept blowing it forward. After watching Kay catch her hair in her free hand and hold on to it, he said softly, **"And forget not that the earth delights to feel your bare feet and the winds long to play with your hair."**

Kay was enchanted by Roy's words. He had a strong romantic streak inside him that she was only now starting to understand. She looked at him quizzically and asked, "Where does that come from? I know that I have read that somewhere before."

Roy flushed slightly and said quietly, "It's a quote from Khalil Gibran. Do you remember that we read some of his poems in our Senior Literature class? I've always liked his work, and that particular quote seemed so perfect for this moment."

Kay and Roy just looked at each other for a long time. They both felt so close to each other after their talk. They poured out a lot of their feelings tonight. Roy still felt that he needed to go slowly with Kay. He thought that perhaps she liked him a little bit, but he didn't want to rush her. If it were up to him, he would tell her that he loved her, and he would ask her to marry him. However, Kay seemed to be dating other guys and hadn't shown that she was ready to hear anything like that from him. Roy's plan was to woo Kay slowly and let her get used to thinking of them as a couple.

Kay remembered that she wanted to tell Roy about her inheritance. "Guess what, Roy?" she asked him quietly.

"What?" he answered just as softly. He still had her hand in his, and now he caressed her wrist lightly.

Kay smilingly looked at their hands and then back at Roy. She loved it when he touched her hand like that. "At the reading of Nana's will this afternoon, I learned that she left me this house and everything in it. I am now a woman with some property." Her words were proud and immensely humble.

Roy smiled kindly at her and said, "Congratulations, Kay. Does this mean that you plan to stay in Litton? You could be a lady of leisure," he gently teased her.

"Oh, no. My parents are anxious to move back to the Chicago area, but they won't go if it means that I'll have to live alone. I hope to get a roommate or two. Then I'll start looking for a nursing job. I heard from some friends of my mom's that Litton Hospital is hiring again. Maybe I'll get a job there. That would be great because it's only seven or eight miles from here. It's time I started living my adult life." Kay spoke determinedly.

"I hope you get whatever job you want. I know that I would be happy if you stayed in town. I like spending time with you. I hope that you will continue to come to the Playhouse and volunteer for the plays. It's so much fun, and the other actors are really great." Roy figured that he would sneak in that bit about liking to spend time with her. If he made clear his interest in her each time he saw her, she might start to think along those lines herself.

There were only two more weeks of rehearsals until they opened to the public. If Kay was not needed to stand in for Letty, she would be allowed to sit in the audience with her father and Martie. Planning to come to the last two weeks of rehearsals, she would get to see Roy each of those days. She hoped that they could continue to get closer and that he would ask her out, just herself, and not her mother, too.

They talked briefly about the play and practices. She told him that she and her mom would be at the next rehearsal. Roy said that he was happy to hear that. As Roy got up to leave, he squeezed her hand gently and bent to kiss her forehead.

"Goodnight, Kay. I hope that you will call me if you want to talk again. I'm here if you need me, okay?" Roy wanted to sweep her into his arms and kiss her goodnight, but he thought that it was too soon. He had enjoyed holding her hand tonight, though. He smiled sweetly at her before he walked down the porch steps.

He heard her say, "Goodnight, Roy, and thanks for everything. You really helped me a lot tonight. See you at rehearsal tomorrow night." At the bottom of the steps, he turned around and waved to her. She waved back and watched him get in his old car and drive away.

Kay went back into her house. Her mom and dad were still talking in the living room. Her mom looked at her intently, but asked innocently, "Did I hear you talking to someone outside, dear?"

"Yes, I was talking with Roy Hillman. When he was here this afternoon, we talked for just a moment. He told me that he had recently lost his beloved grandmother and would be happy to come back and talk with me this evening. He could see how sad I felt about Nana's passing, and he wanted to help. He and I have been talking for an hour, sitting on the porch swing. He just left. I told him that we would be back at rehearsals tomorrow. Oh, he said to give you both his condolences." Kay looked her mom squarely in the eye. She had nothing to hide. Anna liked Roy, too. She would probably be very glad that he had come over and tried to be helpful.

Sterling looked thoughtful. "It was nice of Roy to come over. He seems to be a very nice young man. I'm glad that you have nice friends like him, my dear," he said to Kay. Then he looked at Anna and asked, "You know him pretty well, don't you, love? It seems like you've spoken of him occasionally in the past few years. What do you think of him?"

Anna said, looking between her husband and her daughter, "Roy Hillman is a good man. He has always been kind and considerate whenever he has been at the Playhouse. I've met his mother, too. She seems to be a quiet and very nice woman. I think that Roy will be a good friend for our Kay."

Kay blushed lightly and thought to herself. *If they only knew how I really feel about Roy! Would they approve?* She knew that her parents were not snobs and that having money didn't matter very much to them. *What do they think of Roy's old car?* From the sound of it, he didn't have much extra money to spend on anything. It didn't matter to Kay, but would it matter to her parents, especially if she and Roy started dating? *What if we want to get married? Would Dad still be okay with our relationship?*

Sterling changed the subject and told Kay about the fantastic house that he saw for sale in Chicago. He wanted to take Anna and Kay to look at it. If it was as perfect inside as it had been outside, he might want to move there. Anna would have to love the house too, of course.

He asked Kay if she wanted to stay in Litton. If she wanted to move back to Chicago with them, she would always be welcome in their home. They could either sell Nana's house or rent it out so that Kay had more time to think about what she wanted to do with it.

Kay said that she would love to go to Chicago with them and look at the house, but she planned to live in Litton. She wanted to get a roommate or two and look around for a job in nursing. Chicago was close enough that she could still spend a considerable amount of time there with her parents.

She had many friends in the Chicago area, too. She kept in touch with old junior high and high school friends, as well as those friends that she had made in college. It's just that she needed to stay in Nana's house for a while, maybe a year or two. She could always decide to move back to the Chicago area later.

They went to bed that night tired but feeling able to cope with Nana's death. Sterling planned to call the realtor and see when they could look at that house. In the meantime, he had plenty of work to do at the office in Litton.

Five

Anna and Kay had a quiet day until it was time to go to the Playhouse for rehearsal. It was a hot rainy night, so they carried their umbrellas with them. The air onstage was hot and steamy, so everyone was sweating profusely. Kay noticed that Roy's nice blue polo shirt was sticking to his sweaty back. One drawback of performing in an old theater was the lack of air conditioning. A simple flip of a switch would improve everyone's comfort level. Meanwhile, cast, crew, and director tried to focus on the task at hand and ignore their discomfort.

Kay wished that she could find a way to cool everyone off. Then she remembered seeing a tall oscillating fan at the hardware store a few blocks away. She had been shopping for a few household items when she noticed it. At the time, she wondered if she would need something like that. The house was old and didn't have central air. There were a few window units trying to keep the house cool, but she didn't remember seeing any free-standing fans.

She decided to quickly go to the store and buy it. They could use it tonight and any other night that the stage was so steamy. Then the rest of the time, she could use it in her bedroom. She excused herself and went to get it at the store. After discovering that this model was on sale, she purchased two of them.

"You're an angel!" the director told Kay when she brought in the first fan. She grinned at him and went to set it up. Everyone clustered around it to try to cool off a little. Roy caught her eye and grinned happily at her. She just smiled broadly and said, "I'll just go and get the other one that I bought."

The cast and crew clapped and cheered for her. Roy came toward her and quietly said, "I'll get that other fan for you, Kay. I know that we're all very grateful to you for them."

He walked with her out to her car. Anna and she had come in the Pontiac tonight. She allowed Roy to carry the fan inside. It was kind of heavy, after all. The crowd all came around Kay and thanked her and clapped her on the back for being so smart and generous. Kay just sat back and smiled at all of them. Rehearsal went so much better when everyone felt cooler.

After rehearsal, Roy asked Anna and Kay if they wanted to get a cool beverage someplace before going home. Anna invited Roy to their house, instead. She stated that she had made a big jug of pink lemonade that afternoon and that it would be chilling in the fridge. If she remembered correctly, there were plenty of treats left over from the brunch yesterday, too. She mentioned brownies and little pieces of cheesecake and apple turnovers.

"Anna, you just said the magic words. I love apple turnovers. I grew up with an apple orchard on our farm, and I just love everything to do with apples. My mom makes amazing apple butter and apple pie. Apple turnovers are the next best thing to them. If you're sure, I'd love to come over and have some treats. Lead the way, Madam," Roy said with sudden dramatic flair, as if channeling their beloved director. Both ladies giggled at Roy's surprising levity.

Roy was happy at the prospect of spending a bit more time with Kay. He had been too busy with the rehearsal tonight to say much to her, although he was very aware of her. Roy seemed to know whenever she left the room or went to stand somewhere else.

Kay was excited to have Roy come over for a while. The more time he spent at her house, the better, since she wanted to get to know him better. She wanted her parents to get to know him better, too. He seemed to enjoy his time in Anna's and Kay's company.

Roy spent an enjoyable hour at the Harris' home. He was charming and sweet to the ladies. Sterling was not there; he had a late-night meeting with one of the managers at his office. Still, Roy was careful not to overstay his welcome.

It was cooler now, so Kay took Roy outside to sit on the porch swing. Anna said that she had some telephone calls to make in her bedroom. It was her subtle way of giving Roy and Kay some time alone together.

If it were up to her, Kay and Roy would start dating, maybe fall in love, and even get married. She wanted her Kay to be as happy as she was. Anna had fallen in love with Sterling in high school. They had married young, younger than Kay and Roy were right now.

On the porch, Kay and Roy sat on the swing, talking about the play. Roy held Kay's hand again. He moved a little closer to her until the side of his bare leg touched the side of hers. It was enough to make him get a little tongue-tied. They sat there not speaking much, just content to be with each other. A soft mist arose in the breeze that was now barely perceptible but nonetheless refreshing.

Roy squeezed Kay's hand and then lifted it to his lips. He gently kissed her hand and looked her in the eyes. "I enjoy spending time with you, Kay. Thank you for letting me come over tonight. I'll see you in a few days, right?"

Kay felt butterflies in her stomach at his sweet kiss on her hand. *Roy was so romantic,* she thought happily. She smiled very sweetly at him and said, "Thank you for coming over. I enjoy spending time with you, too. Yes, Mom and I will be there at the next rehearsal. Have a safe trip home, Roy."

He nodded and departed the Harris' home from the front porch. As he descended the four wooden steps, he felt the drizzling rain and reveled in its coolness. Kay remained on the swing for a while longer, watching Roy drive away. Her mom came out to see if Roy was still there. She sat on the swing with Kay and looked at her. To her loving eyes, she thought that her baby was in love.

"You really like Roy, don't you, honey?" Anna gently asked her daughter.

Kay looked at her mom with stars still in her eyes and nodded. "I think that I'm in love with him, Mom," Kay answered her mom quietly.

Anna grabbed Kay's hand and squeezed it. "Do you really, Kay? I hope that things go well for both of you. Do you know how Roy feels about you?"

"Oh, I think he likes me, too. He is a quiet man, but a very romantic one. He just kissed my hand before he left and told me that he likes spending time with me. I like that, too. I have never been in love before. I think that he's so wonderful. I wish that I could be with him all the time."

Kay couldn't suppress her happy smile. Roy was going slowly, but each moment they spent together, he left her with a feeling that he was liking her more and more. Maybe he needed to go slowly for some reason. Well, Kay would be there, just waiting for Roy to ask her out.

Anna quietly talked with Kay for ten more minutes. She told Kay that she would do anything to help her. She liked Roy a lot and thought that Kay and he would make a lovely couple. She encouraged Kay not to get discouraged. Some men liked to take their time when they courted a girl. Maybe Roy was one of those men. Kay agreed and said that she was fine—she was not discouraged. In fact, after that sweet kiss on the hand, she felt closer to Roy than ever before.

Anna said, "Goodnight, love. Don't stay out here too long. You know how much the mosquitos love sweet things!" Both laughed, and Anna went inside while Kay remained outside on the swing.

Like the soft rain around her, Nana's wise words gently fell from her memory into conscious thought. *If Roy and I are meant to be together, we will be.*

Just then, the wind picked up and there was a brilliant flash, followed by distant thunder. Kay laughed, saying aloud, "Okay, Nana—I hear you!" Then, more quietly, " . . . and I miss you . . . so very, very much. How I wish you could meet Roy. You'd love him, Nana . . . I know I do."

*   *   *

Kay brought both of her oscillating fans with her to the next rehearsal, just in case it was stifling hot again. It was indeed a warm night, and the director was glad that she brought them in. He asked her to set them up. Not able to contain his glee, he once again entertained the assembled with an impromptu dramatic scene.

"Oh, fair maiden who brings with her the heavenly tempests!
Leave not this place nor ignore this merry band of actors' requests:
Set these winds to blow 'cross the stage hither and yon
And cool the countenances that these breezes fall upon.
Turn not away from our heated work 'til such work be done
And the audience cries 'Encore!' again for everyone."

Thus spent, the director bowed.

Again, an immense applause arose from the cast and crew as they cheered both Kay and the director. Someone found artificial flowers and threw them onstage at the director's feet.

Touched, he grasped the flowers to his bosom and gave another deep bow. It was all so much fun.

The fans blew Kay's hair around, and she was reminded about Roy's romantic quote from Khalil Gibran. She looked up and saw Roy watching her. From the look on his face, he remembered it, too. He grinned quickly at her and then turned away as the director called to him.

After rehearsal was over, Roy convinced Anna and Kay that they should let him buy them a cone at the Dairy Queen. They acquiesced and met him there. Roy saw a few guys that he knew there, again. They teased him that this was the second time in several weeks that they had seen him with some lovely ladies. He good-naturedly introduced them to Anna and Kay. His hand under Kay's elbow silently said to them, "Back off, this girl is with me."

Anna and Kay enjoyed the openly flirtatious behavior of Roy's acquaintances. Kay liked the slightly possessive vibe that Roy was giving off about her to them. She wouldn't have minded shouting out, "I'm with Roy! He's mine." Of course, she did no such thing. After an hour at the Dairy Queen, she and Anna reluctantly said their goodbyes and left.

With only one week of rehearsals left before the opening night, the actors were a little uptight and stressed. The sets were done, and the opening night show was sold out. Kay bought tickets for her father and Martie. They had end-of-the-front row seats. That way Kay would be close enough for the director to come and get her if she was needed.

Martie planned to stay with Kay for a day or so. They talked on the telephone once a week. Martie remained curious about the identity and status of the girl Roy liked. At every opportunity, she reminded him that he had better have her at the show.

Kay had not told Martie that she was in love with Roy. She knew that Martie periodically talked with Roy. Martie was the type of girl to tell Roy about Kay's crush on him if she thought that it would do any good. No, it was far better to say nothing to her about Roy.

It was the first week in September, and the weather was still delightful. It was the beginning of harvest time on the Hillman farm, so Roy wasn't sure if his parents or brothers would come to the show. He invited them and told them that he would buy their tickets if they wanted to come. His mom reluctantly told him that his father was so busy and expected Tom and John to help him out, but she was able to come. Roy made sure that he got her a good seat.

On the night of the show, Kay was still not needed to stand in for Letty, so she took her seat in the audience. She sat between her father and Martie. She didn't realize that they both watched her face as much as they watched the play. Anna did a wonderful job with her role. Kay and Sterling were very proud of her. Kay's eyes didn't waver from Roy during his scenes. She had both a look of pride and of love on her face when she watched him. Sterling and Martie exchanged glances with raised eyebrows. *This is very interesting,* they both thought.

Kay clapped as hard as everyone else when the play was over. She took Martie and Sterling behind the curtains to introduce them to the cast. The cast was feeling ecstatic because the play was a resounding success. The director was walking around, complimenting the cast on their wonderful rendition of the play and, of course, waxing poetic as he did so. They had two additional shows within the next few days, but the opening night was always the most dramatic and special to the cast.

Everyone was hugging and kissing one another. Roy was standing next to Letty. He had just hugged her and kissed her cheek. Their shared scenes had gone perfectly. They had an air of closeness about them. After all, they had just successfully played their parts as a married couple.

Martie saw that and made the incorrect assumption that Letty was the girl that Roy liked. He was shy about hugging and kissing Kay. With Martie and Sterling there, he felt like he should just be casually friendly. He hugged Martie, who laughed at him and said that she would only be satisfied with a kiss. She kissed him full on the lips. He flushed a bit and laughingly said something funny back to her.

Kay stood by and looked on quietly. She would have liked to have a hug and kiss from Roy, but it seemed as if he didn't want that. She was a little confused. She thought that he was starting to like her and would be asking her out one of these days. Her pride was a little hurt. When he looked at her, she gave him a cool look back. If he really didn't want to be with her, she would pretend to not want to be with him either.

Roy frowned. Something was the matter. He could feel Kay's coolness toward him. Maybe she didn't want Martie or her father seeing her being friendly with him for some reason. He wasn't sure what he should do about the situation. Maybe nothing—maybe everything would go back to normal when Martie and her father left. Kay had told him that they were only coming to the opening night show. He would have to hope that Kay would be her sweet friendly self at the next two shows.

Later, Martie and Kay discussed the play. Martie was spending the next day with the Harris family and driving back to Chicago on the following morning. She had a full-time job nursing in a big hospital in Glencoe. She still lived with her parents but was looking for a nice apartment to rent.

Martie was careful not to say too much about Roy. From what she saw, Kay still really liked Roy, but he apparently liked that other cast member. Martie felt terrible for her best friend. They spent an enjoyable day together—shopping and talking about nothing much. She left the next morning after giving Kay a huge hug and a peppy salute. She said that she would call again next week, and they would talk again.

Kay had no idea that Martie was feeling bad about her and her crush on Roy. She didn't know that her father was feeling that way, too. Anna had not yet told Sterling about Kay's confession of love for Roy. She wanted to give Kay more time with Roy before she talked about him to her husband. If Sterling knew that Kay was in love with Roy, he might feel tempted to do something about it. In Anna's experience, men—especially her man—were "fixers". They felt the compunction to "fix" whatever was making their lady, or in this case, daughter, unhappy.

That evening, the play had its second performance. Kay watched the play with her usual care. She was careful to look at Roy with no expression when they met after the play's completion. She was still a bit hurt that Roy had not hugged or kissed her when he had done that to most of the female cast members. In her mind, the ball was in his court.

Once again, Roy felt Kay's coolness, but he didn't know what to do. He had never had a girlfriend or experienced a feeling of her being upset with him. An experienced man would have known how to make his girlfriend happy again, but Roy was stymied about knowing how to handle it. He smiled gently at her, but Kay did not smile back.

There was only one show left, and then the Playhouse would be empty for a few weeks. Roy didn't know how he would be able to keep seeing Kay after tomorrow. If she was upset with him, she would certainly not want him to come over to her house and talk. Roy couldn't do anything except let her see that he was not upset with her at all. He would be as friendly as he could.

He walked up to her, smiled warmly, and asked quietly, "How did you like tonight's show, Kay? I thought that we did a good job. It's not quite as exciting as opening night, but it was still a good show, right?"

Kay looked up at him with hooded eyes. She nodded and said carefully, "Yes, the show was just as good as it was the other day. I'm happy for the cast that it went so well." She stopped talking and stood there watching him quietly.

Roy felt like he had to say something, so he asked, "Did Martie get back home okay? It was good to see her again. She is such a fun person. I hope she liked the play."

"Oh, she liked it. She said that all of you were terrific—especially you. If you ever gave her any sign, she would jump at the chance to be your girlfriend, you know." Kay's voice was quiet and subdued.

Roy didn't know how to respond to that. "Umm, thank you. She told me that a long time ago. I apologized to her and told her that there was someone else. Can you guess who the girl is that I like, Kay?" Roy's heart was pounding. He hoped that Kay would figure it out.

Roy was supremely disappointed when Kay just shook her head and remained quiet. *What had gone wrong?* Roy asked himself. He thought that they were starting to get somewhere, and that Kay was beginning to see that he really liked her. He was frustrated and getting a bit angry, too.

He kept his frustration out of his voice and said cheerfully, "Well, I hope that we'll have another good show tomorrow night. I'll talk with you again tomorrow after the show, okay? Have a great evening, Kay." He gently touched her shoulder and smiled nicely at her before turning and walking away.

Kay wondered if he was trying to make amends. He certainly seemed to be trying to be friendly toward her. Was he only being friendly because they were friends, or did he like her more than that? She was so confused and unhappy. She would have to wait and see what would happen the next night. It would be the last time that she would see him for a while.

If he decided not to come over to her house, she wouldn't see him for weeks, until they started to rehearse for the next play. She still had no idea where he lived. She didn't even have his telephone number. The ball really was in his court.

He knew where she lived. If he didn't choose to come and see her, she guessed that she had been making too much out of his hand holding and compliments. Maybe he only wanted to be friends and nothing more.

Sadness darkened Kay's face as she rode home with her mom. Anna could see that Kay was upset and preoccupied. "If you want to talk about whatever is wrong, just let me know, okay, honey? I'm here for you no matter what time it is—night or day. I love you, Kay." Anna's voice was loving and gentle. Kay just nodded but kept silent. She wanted to think about things some more.

That night Kay pulled out her old yearbook and looked through it. She zeroed in on Roy's graduation picture. *Wow, he was quite thin,* she thought. She looked at the pictures of him running in his track clothes. She read that he took first and second place a few times.

Then she remembered that he had written some words of wisdom on her autograph pages. She remembered that she had written in his book as well, telling him to be strong and courageous. She still didn't know why she wrote that inscription in his book, other than it was part of a Bible verse that she had always liked.

She found his inscription for her. Now she remembered—it was a quote or two from Mother Teresa. She had read it the day he wrote it but hadn't given it much thought, other than that it sounded like something Roy would say.

Kay tried to remember back to her days in high school with him. Even though she had never thought about going out with him, she had always admired Roy Hillman. He was smart and interesting. He had a nice face. She had always wondered why he never smiled in high school. He was always kind to her and sweet. She remembered challenging him that she was going to beat his scores on their assignments.

There had been a few times when she had done that, and she teased him. He had never gotten angry with her. In fact, she had never seen him angry with anyone. He had always just been a very nice and kind person. Now she re-read his inscription to her. **"Yesterday is gone. Tomorrow has not yet come. We have only today. Let us begin. Every time you smile at someone, it is an action of love, a gift to that person, a beautiful thing."**

Did that quote have a hidden meaning? Had he thought that her smile was beautiful? She wished that she had paid more attention to him in high school. Because she was so focused on going to college, she hadn't wanted to get close to any boy. That included the boys that she had dated.

Had Roy liked her in high school? If so, she felt ashamed of the casual way she had treated him. Here she was four years later, head over heels in love with him. If only she had known how she would feel about him one day, she would have been nicer to him.

That thought made her sad. She shook herself; she had to get a grip on herself. Not all was lost. Maybe Roy would do something that would show her that he had some feelings for her after all. It was time to break out of this apathy that she felt. That was not who she was; she was a happy person.

Six

The next evening, Kay watched the play and clapped along with everyone else. She ran behind the stage when it was over and gave her mom a big hug. The cast did a phenomenal job tonight. They were all so happy. The cast party would be held at the director's house across town. Kay would be attending it with her mom. She waited around to see if she could help with the props and the set. After everyone had the sets cleared and props put in the storage room, the cast started to leave for the party. Roy had given Kay a sunny smile when he saw her but hadn't spoken to her. She hoped that he would talk with her tonight at the party.

The party was in full swing when Kay and her mom got there. They had gone home first to change clothes. Sterling wasn't home yet, so they left him a note and went to the party. Kay drove them in her Pontiac. When they got there, they greeted the director and thanked him for the invitation. He waved them over to the drinks and snacks table. Since Kay was driving, she only took a soft drink.

She saw Roy standing in the corner talking with Letty. He had his hand on her arm and was talking animatedly. She was smiling at him. Kay wondered if they had gotten close during all those rehearsals. They certainly looked like they were intent on each other. Kay felt more confused than ever. *Is Roy not interested in me at all?* She had felt sure that he was. She was just waiting for him to ask her out. What if that was not to be the case?

Kay skirted around them and started to talk to some of the other cast members. She listened when the director loudly announced that he would be at the Playhouse in three weeks with a selection of new plays for them to look through. Until then, he was taking some time off, and he urged them all to do the same.

After an hour, Kay and Roy still had not spoken to each other. He was always talking to someone else when she walked past him. She could feel his eyes on her, though. It seemed like every time she looked toward him, he was looking at her. He smiled at her numerous times.

Anna was tired and asked Kay if they could leave in ten minutes or so. Kay reluctantly agreed. Maybe she would never get the chance to say anything to Roy tonight. Anna and she were making the rounds, saying goodnight, when Roy fetched up next to her. He was looking very thoughtful. He smiled at her and went to gently hug her. He said a quiet goodnight. As he turned away, he started to speak quietly in French.

Kay had to strain to hear him, but she ended up hearing every word clearly. *"Et c'est dans un regard, dans un sourire que sont cachés les mots qu'on n'a jamais su dire."* With those words uttered, he continued to slowly walk away.

Kay knew exactly what he had quietly said. She spoke fluent French. Roy probably didn't know it, but Kay had gone to a French immersion school in elementary school. She had taken French in Junior High and in Senior High. Roy had quietly said, *"And it is in a look, in a smile, that are hidden the words that we never knew how to say."*

What had he meant? Kay wondered. She turned to her mom, who was preparing to leave, and said, "Mom, I need to talk to Roy for a bit. Can you wait a little longer before we leave?"

Anna didn't show it, but she was glad to hear this. *At least they're still talking*, she thought to herself. Then, replying, "Okay. Good luck, honey."

Kay went outside to stand beside Roy's car. It was a nice evening, and she relished the warm night air as she leaned against his car waiting for him to show up. He came out of the door about six minutes later, walking slowly. He didn't notice her until he was nearly at his driver's side door. He looked up, startled at seeing her there.

"What words did you never know how to say, Roy?" Kay asked him very quietly. Roy looked nonplussed for a minute and then reluctantly grinned.

"I should have known that you would speak French, Kay. You do so many things well." Roy wasn't sure how to go on. He had been thinking those words, and they had slipped out. He often said things to himself in French because he tried to maintain his French skills.

"Do you have some time to talk, Kay?" He asked her quietly. Now was the time to tell her that he liked her. Maybe it was too soon to tell her that he loved her, but they could go forward with 'like'.

"Yes, I would like to talk with you, Roy. Will you come over to my house this evening to talk with me?" she asked him, just as quietly.

He thought about that for a few seconds. "Well, it's kind of personal. Do you think that we could go somewhere else where we could have some privacy? No offense meant to your parents, but I don't think that I could talk openly knowing that your parents might come out and interrupt us at any minute. Can you understand, Kay? I'm wondering if you would mind talking with me at my apartment. I promise that you will be safe." Roy was earnest.

Kay smiled when he said that. She felt very safe with Roy. She knew in her heart that Roy would never do anything to hurt her. She was fine with his suggestion because she wanted to see Roy's apartment, anyway.

"Let me take my mom home first. Why don't you follow me back to my house so I can do that? Then I'll follow you to your apartment. If I drive there, it'll save you the trouble of having to drive me back home." She wanted to be practical and helpful to him.

"It's no trouble driving you back to your house, but if you'd rather have your own car, I guess I don't mind. I'll wait for you in my car. Why don't you go and get your mom and explain to her what the plan is, okay? And thank you, Kay, for agreeing to talk with me." Roy's voice was soft.

Kay agreed. She went indoors to get her mom. When she explained to her mom, Anna nodded agreement.

"That's fine, honey. I'm glad that you two are finally going to talk. It seems like it is long overdue. Do you want me to wait up for you, so we can talk when you get home?" Anna questioned her.

"No, Mom, but plan to talk with me tomorrow morning after Dad leaves for work. I have no idea what Roy wants to say to me, but I'm praying for something positive." Kay smiled at her mom.

She kissed her mom at their door and followed Roy to his apartment. When she saw where they ended up, she felt sorry that Roy had to live there. *These are very shabby apartments,* she thought. Perhaps he couldn't afford anything else. Well, it still didn't matter to Kay one little bit. She probably loved him even more because of it. He obviously tried hard to make his salary work for him.

Roy led her inside his apartment. It was quiet and dark inside. He turned on the living room lights and sat her down on his most comfortable chair. He took the other one and pulled it close to hers. After he got them both a cold soft drink from the fridge, he sat down and cleared his throat. *It's now or never,* he thought.

He gently took her hand in his and looked tenderly at her. "Kay, I have wanted to tell you for a long time that I really like you. I've liked you ever since high school. I think that you are so beautiful, sweet, and kind. I like your quick intellect and your outgoing personality. I'm sure that you never knew in high school that I had a crush on you. I was just happy that we talked sometimes. When Martie asked me if I liked her, I told her that I liked someone else. I was talking about you. I've never really had a girlfriend before, and I wanted to go slow. I didn't want you to feel uncomfortable around me. I thought that we were getting closer lately, but last week you seemed to change. You looked like you suddenly disliked me. I didn't know what to do. There, now you know. Our future relationship is up to you."

Kay just smiled very widely. What a relief it was to hear that! She had been praying that Roy liked her. She would show him that she liked him, too. She would have to be careful not to show him her love, though. Maybe he was not ready for that.

"Thank you for telling me, Roy. No, I couldn't tell that you had a crush on me in high school. You were always so serious, and you never smiled. I admired you and thought that you were so nice. I'm very sorry if I hurt you in any way, Roy. I tried not to get involved with any boy in high school. I knew that I wanted to go to college, and I didn't want to be held back like some of the girls in our class. They gave up what they wanted to do in life because they didn't want to leave their boyfriends to go to college or whatever." Kay was speaking earnestly. She still had a lot to explain. After so much time waiting, it was tempting to let all her thoughts and emotions cascade in an avalanche of words. Still, she knew that she had to be patient.

"When I came back to Litton and met you again, I was instantly attracted to you. I still am. I would go on dates with you if you asked me, Roy," Kay shyly revealed.

Roy reached over and kissed Kay for the very first time. Kay warmly accepted his lips and pressed back in kind. They broke apart and smiled at each other.

Despite Roy's shyness, and lack of experience with such matters, Kay thought that their first kiss was wonderful. He had put so much feeling into it.

"That was even better than I had hoped it would be, Kay," Roy murmured breathlessly. He was eager to kiss her again.

Kay smiled serenely and said, "Thank you, Roy. That was a wonderful kiss. I liked it very much. You have such nice lips."

Roy asked her, "Would it be okay if we started dating? I would like to take you out to places, and just spend quiet evenings talking and listening to music, too. Do you like that idea?"

Kay said agreeably, "Yes, Roy, I would like that, too. We don't always have to go places. I would be happy to spend time with you either here or at my house. I can sometimes pay for our dates, too.

After all, these are the 70s. We modern girls don't mind taking our dates out occasionally." She flashed him an impish grin.

"I don't know about that, Kay. I can afford to take you out. Let me explain something to you. I could afford to live somewhere nicer than this, but I deliberately chose to live in the least expensive apartment that I could find. I have been saving my money so that I can buy a house by the time I'm twenty-six. I keep my old car for the same reason. It works great, and I don't care what people say about it. If it still runs, why get a new one?"

Kay thought that Roy was smart for making his plans and sticking to them—and she told him so. Thus began a lengthy discussion of everything from family to dreams, jobs, Litton, friends, the Playhouse, and more.

Kay realized that they had been talking for three hours. She was certain that her parents were waiting up to make sure she got home safely. She told him that, and he apologized for keeping her for so long. He walked her to the door of his apartment and took her in his arms. This time he was more confident and gave her a wonderful kiss, long and lingering. Kay kissed him back, just as enthusiastically.

He walked her out to her car and helped her get in. Then he gave her one more quick kiss and asked her if he could come over to her house the next evening at seven pm. She smilingly agreed and waved to him when she drove away.

On her way home, she thought about tonight. She was so happy that Roy liked her and wanted to date her. *If only he loved me,* she thought with a little sadness. She was ready to marry him, but it might take him some time to grow to love her. She just had to be patient. At least he wanted to date her.

Roy thought about the evening after Kay left. He felt good that she enjoyed his kisses. He was a little shy about kissing her. He wanted them to be perfect and for her to enjoy them. Well, she seemed to enjoy them, especially that second kiss. She had kissed him back, too. He grinned as he recalled the way she kissed him back.

Then he sobered a bit. He was still going to have to take things slowly. She liked him, but she didn't love him yet. Maybe after they dated for six months, he would be able to tell her that he loved her. He would have to wait and see how she reacted to him. He planned to do everything right. She hadn't explained why she had been so cool towards him, but maybe it didn't matter anymore. Roy went to bed happy that night.

The next morning after Sterling left the house, Anna and Kay got comfortable on the couch in the living room. Anna waited until Kay was ready to start talking. Kay looked shyly at her mom as she unconsciously stroked the pillow that lived on the couch.

"We talked for a long time at Roy's apartment last night. He told me that he has liked me since we were in high school. He asked if I had known that he had a crush on me then, but I didn't. Roy was nice in school, but he was always so serious and intense. When I met him again in June, I found him quite attractive. He seemed so different from what he was like in high school. I guess that I was just too immature to see how great he was, even back then. Anyway, he wants us to date. I told him that I would like that, too." Kay spoke quietly to her mom.

"But honey, did you tell him that you are in love with him?" asked Anna carefully.

Kay shook her head no and said, "No, Mom. I'll be fine just dating him for now. Maybe in a little while, he'll come to love me, too. Nana always said that you can't force someone to love you. She said that I should show my love through actions instead of words. I plan to show Roy that I care about him through my actions. Nana also said that men liked to do their own chasing in their own way. If Roy's way is to go slowly, then that's what I'll do, too. I'm just so happy that we finally talked, and he admitted to me that he likes me. I can work with that."

She smiled softly when she remembered Roy's second kiss. For a young man who hadn't kissed girls very often, he kissed her very well, indeed.

They talked about the possibility of Kay getting a job in town. Kay also wanted to advertise for a roommate. Even though her father had not said that he wanted to move to Chicago right away, Kay sensed that he was making secret plans. She wanted to have things fairly settled so that Sterling and Anna could move without having any worries about her.

That afternoon, dressed formally in a nice blue suit and silk blouse, Kay drove to the Litton Hospital to see if she could get a job there. As she was waiting in a little room to talk with someone, she looked up and saw her old high school friend, Debra. Debbie, as she preferred to be called, was dressed in a Litton Hospital uniform. She smiled widely at Kay.

"Kay Harris, is that you? It's good to see you. I had not heard that you were back in Litton. What are you doing here?" Debbie's voice was friendly and questioning.

"Hi, Debbie. It's good to see you, too. Yes, I came back to Litton in June. I finished my training and am now a Registered Nurse. I came here hoping to get a job. How about you? It looks like you beat me to it." Kay smiled at her old friend.

"Me? Oh, I'm a Licensed Practical Nurse. I've been working here for more than a year. It's a pretty good job. I'm only planning on working full time until I get married. Do you remember Donny Litman? Well, we've been going out for a few years. We're getting married next May." Debbie smiled broadly when she talked about her Donny.

"Congratulations, Debbie. Yes, I remember Donny. You had a crush on him even back in high school, didn't you?" Kay paused because those words made her think of Roy.

Debbie grinned, "Yes, I have been writing Mrs. Donny Litman in my notebook since I was sixteen, I think. I guess I knew a good thing when I saw it, right? How about you? Are you married or engaged? It seems like you should be—all the boys were crazy about you in high school."

Kay shook her head no and lightly said, "No, I wanted to concentrate on college. I've lived in Chicago with my uncle's family for the past four years. I sort of had blinders on, so I didn't get too focused on any boy. I'm just back in Litton, and I haven't seen many people yet. I'm not in any hurry." Kay apologized in her head to Roy. She was certainly focused on him right now.

"Well, good luck with the job hunting. I think that I heard that they were going to add another RN position in the future. Just think, you could be my boss." Debbie grinned again as she looked at Kay.

Kay smiled back at her and sat back down to wait for the medical secretary to talk with her.

Before Debbie left the room, she suddenly asked Kay, "I don't suppose you've heard about anyone needing a roommate, have you? I don't want to get an apartment unless necessary. They usually require you to live there for a whole year. My wedding is on the 2nd of May, and I don't want to pay for months that I'm not planning to live there. Donny and I are going to live in his parents' house. As soon as we get married, his parents will be moving to Florida. They have some relatives there, and they like that climate better. Regarding a roommate situation, I only want somewhere to lay my head at night. I'm not home very much, so I only need a bedroom. Let me give you my number in case you hear of anything, okay?"

Kay thought for just a second before hurriedly saying, "I'm looking for a roommate. I've just inherited my Nana's house, and my parents are itching to move back to Chicago. I know that my dad and mom won't move until I have a roommate or two. My big old house has five bedrooms, and I'll rattle around in it without someone else living there. How about moving in with me? I would love to have you in the house." Kay looked at Debbie with hopeful anticipation.

"Oh, wow! That would be great. If I remember correctly, your house is less than ten miles away from the hospital, right?" Debbie was starting to get a little excited. "I want to move out of my parents' house. It's so crowded there. If you remember, I have five younger brothers and sisters. I'm old enough to be on my own. How much do you charge for rent?" Debbie sat back down to talk some more with Kay.

Kay and Debbie talked for fifteen more minutes and agreed on a reasonable rent. Kay didn't really need the rent money, but Debbie told her that the price she was charging was very fair. They planned for Debbie to move in next week on her days off. Her dad, brothers, and Donny would help her move her things. She only had her clothes and some personal items to move, so it didn't appear to be that big of a production.

They exchanged telephone numbers and promised to talk again the following day. Then Debbie had to go. She was supposed to stop at the grocery store and pick up a few things for her mom for their supper. She stopped to give Kay a big hug before she rushed off. Kay was ecstatic that one of the big things on her 'to do' list was taken care of. If she could only get a job as easily, she would be set.

Kay saw the medical secretary and handed over her credentials. The secretary had been working at the hospital for many years and knew all the families living in Litton. Kay got reacquainted with her. She promised to give Kay's application and resume to her superiors, and they would let Kay know if they wanted to interview her.

Kay stopped off at the big new grocery store on her way home. She hoped that she would get a glimpse of Roy. She didn't know that his office was on the second floor, way in the back of the store. She wandered through the store, picking up a few things to bring home. Her mom usually did the grocery shopping, but Kay was going to have to get used to doing it. Soon her parents would move out, and Kay would have to do all the housekeeping herself.

She was glad that she had run into Debbie today. *We will be good roommates,* Kay thought. Debbie was a friendly girl and really kind. They should get along just fine.

Kay told her parents the good news about Debbie at supper. She said that she was hoping to get a job at the hospital. According to the medical secretary and Debbie, the hospital was planning to hire some new staff. Her resume and credentials were top-notch, so she was hopeful that they would interview her.

She told them that Roy was coming over at 7:00 pm to talk with her. Kay blushed prettily when she said that. Her parents looked at her with love. They liked Roy and hoped that Kay and he would fall in love and get married.

Roy came over with a pretty bunch of flowers for Kay. He went into the house and said hello to Anna and Sterling. He knew Anna much better than Kay's father. Kay had mentioned that her dad was a sweetie, so Roy was not too nervous around him. Because Roy was interested in so many things, Sterling and he talked easily for a few minutes before he turned back to Kay and smiled at her.

"Do you want to talk on the swing, Kay? It's such a beautiful night." Roy was flatteringly attentive to her. He glanced quickly at her parents and smiled.

"Yes, let's go out on the swing. I want to tell you about my news. And you can tell me how your day went, too." Kay gave her parents a quick smile and took Roy's hand to lead him outside.

She told him about meeting up with Debbie and asking her to be her roommate. They talked about Donny and Debbie and a few other classmates. Kay told him about the possibility of getting a job at the Litton Hospital. Roy was very supportive of everything that Kay was excited about. He told her a little bit about his day. It had been a regular day—not much to report.

As they sat on the swing, Roy held her hand and smiled at her frequently. Their relationship was so new that they still had quite a few things to talk about. He was just the tiniest bit formal with Kay. She hoped that he would relax a little bit more and just be himself with her. To encourage him, she snuggled right up to him and laid her head on his shoulder.

Roy was surprised but quite pleased. He put his arm around her and laid his head down to rest lightly on her head. They sat quietly in the dark, listening to the cicadas and other night creatures. The wind was soft and fragrant. The swing moved slowly back and forth with the steady movement of Roy's long legs. It was very peaceful. Roy felt content and happy. If they could date like this for a few months, he thought that by Christmas he would be able to tell Kay that he loved her.

Kay was very relaxed and content, as well. They didn't always have to talk. Sometimes it was nice to just be with each other without even having to say a word. They sat in companionable silence for half an hour before Roy stirred. He had an early day tomorrow, so he should think about going home. His arm tightened on Kay's shoulder, and he turned her toward him. He looked at her beautiful face in the dark and immersed himself in her luminous eyes.

Roy bent and gently kissed Kay's lips. He was happy to feel her lips press back against his. They kissed for a minute before he reluctantly pulled away from her. *I definitely like kissing Kay,* he thought with a soft smile. As he rose from the swing, he felt a little lightheaded. He gently pulled Kay up so that she was standing, too. Putting his long arms around her, he gently hugged her before giving her a quick kiss on top of her pretty hair. Roy quietly said goodnight and told her that he would call her the next evening. Kay nodded and shyly waved goodbye to him as he got in his car to go home.

CHAPTER

Seven

The next evening, when he came home from work, Roy was surprised and concerned to see Johnny sitting on the outside steps of the apartment building with a beat-up suitcase next to him. Roy ran up to him and sat down on the steps next to him.

"Johnny, what's wrong? Are you okay? What about Dad, Mom, and Tom?" Roy's voice was a little anxious. Ever since Roy moved out while he was in his first year in college, Johnny had never visited. *Why is he here now?* Roy wondered.

Johnny's young face was somber and a little frightened. He looked at his older brother and said, "You told me to come to you if I ever needed to talk. I need to talk. Do you have time for me right now?" His voice was a little shaky.

Roy said, "Of course, I have time to talk with you, Johnny. Come on in and get comfortable. How did you get here?"

"Tom brought me over after school today. I told him that I was either going to run away or come to talk with you. I brought another set of clothes, just in case you allowed me to stay overnight tonight." Johnny followed Roy up to his apartment.

Since it is only a one-bedroom apartment, I will have to put Johnny on the couch tonight, Roy thought. His single bed was too small for them to share. He would offer to take the couch, but it was much too short for his six-foot-four frame. Johnny was shorter—a mere five-foot-ten-inches tall. Either way, whoever slept on the couch would have an uncomfortable night.

Roy placed Johnny's suitcase near the couch. He gave him a cold soft drink and led him into the living room. Directing his younger brother to sit down on the couch, Roy announced, "Now, why don't you start from the beginning? Remember that I will not judge you, Johnny, no matter what you have to say. You're my little brother, and I love you."

Johnny was visibly uncomfortable by his older brother's proclamation of love. He was not used to anyone telling him that they loved him. In his opinion, his family was not very demonstrative.

"I know that you were shy in high school. I was only about ten or eleven, but I remember that you used to have a huge crush on Kayleen Harris. How did you ever get over that?" Johnny was earnest and serious.

Roy was caught somewhat off guard by the question. "Why do you want to know, Johnny? That was six or seven years ago."

Johnny looked down at his hands. They were clenched on his lap. "I think that I have the same problem. There is this girl in my homeroom class. Her name is Caroline Humphries. She sits in the row next to me. She has pale blonde hair that reminds me of cornsilk. It's long and silky looking. She wears wire-rimmed round glasses and is slim. Her pretty eyes are blue. I get to see them every day because she takes off her glasses and cleans them on a little piece of cloth during homeroom. If I turn in my seat just a little, I can see her face when she does that. She always looks around the room to see if anyone is watching, so I pretend that I'm looking at something else. The other guys in my class don't think that she is pretty, but I do. I think that I love her. I can hardly breathe anytime she talks to me. My heart starts to beat so fast that I feel like I will pass out."

Roy smiled inwardly. Yep, that was how he felt about Kay when he saw her in their homeroom class. He felt bad for his little brother. It was a heck of a way to have to get through every day at school. He let Johnny talk until he was talked out. Then he thought that he would tell Johnny about Kay. He had not yet spoken about her to his family. No one knew that they were dating. He suspected that his mom knew that he was still interested in Kay, but he never came right out and told her.

"It's funny that you should bring up Kay Harris. I never got over my crush on her. She's back in Litton now. I met up with her by accident a few months ago. I never told any of you, but she joined the Litton Playhouse group, and we saw each other at rehearsals several times a week. We got to be friends. Her grandmother just passed away a few weeks ago, and I went over to talk with her. You know how bad I felt when Grandma Royal passed away last year, right? Well, I just went to talk with her so she would feel better. We've been dating ever since then. I see her most evenings at her house for an hour or two. It's a new relationship, but I think it's going well."

Roy wasn't sure if he wanted to tell anyone that he loved Kay and intended to marry her.

Johnny's jaw dropped down, "Really? Wow, you sure kept that under your hat, Roy. Why didn't you tell any of us about that?"

Roy shrugged. "I guess that I wasn't ready to talk about her to all of you. Now, how do you want me to help you with Caroline, Johnny?"

Johnny looked uncomfortable again. "First of all, would you just call me John? I'm too old to still be called Johnny. And second, how did you learn how to talk with girls? Not just Caroline, but with other girls, too? If you're dating Kay, you must have found a way to talk with her."

Roy nodded. He understood about his brother wanting a more adult name. He could easily call him John from now on. He would even stress to his parents and Tom that John was older now and wanted to have an adult name. He realized that he would have loved to have a trusted older boy give him advice about girls. Then it wouldn't have taken him until the age of twenty-two to get over his shyness.

"That's another funny thing, John. I didn't learn how to start talking to girls until June of this year. I was with Kay, her mom, and her friend, Martie, at the Dairy Queen after rehearsal one night. Kay and Martie were openly flirting with me. I just let myself relax and mimicked what they did. They said some clever things in a flirtatious voice, and I tried it, too. It was so much fun. The next day I tried flirting with a cute salesclerk, and it worked again. She gave me her name and telephone number and told me to call her. It was amazing. If I would have known how to do that in high school, things could have been so different for me. Of course, I probably needed to go through everything that I did in high school and college to make me into the man I am now. But you're different than I was. You're strong and good-looking. You could probably pull off being a flirt." Roy looked at John speculatively.

John looked away and then back at Roy and abruptly said, "I'm too fat. I want to lose weight and be more fit. Caroline is so slim. She wouldn't want to go out with me even if I had enough nerve to ask her out. Will you help me lose weight, Roy? You've always been thin. How can I get thin, too?"

"Well, John, I had the opposite problem. I was downright skinny in high school. None of the girls seemed to want to go out with me, either. Once I was in college, I took a Health class and learned how to use weights to build up my upper and lower body. I'll bet that you can use them to slim down, too. Why don't we try that? I still have my old weight-lifting set around here someplace. Maybe we can work out together. You should probably also watch what you eat, too. Try to eat less fat and salt. If you talked with Mom, I think that she would serve some things that are less fatty and salty. It's not good for Dad or Tom, either. Both are a bit overweight." Roy was starting to get really interested in this discussion. He would like to help his dad and brothers to be more fit.

Roy suddenly remembered that he was supposed to be at Kay's house right now. She didn't call him, but she was probably sitting on her porch swing just waiting for him to come over.

"Excuse me, John. I need to call Kay. I was supposed to be there half an hour ago. Why don't you look in my fridge and see if I have anything that would be good for supper, okay?" Roy was anxious to talk with Kay and tell her why he was late.

Anna answered the telephone. Roy quickly told her that he had an unexpected visit from his younger brother and that he was still at his apartment. He asked to speak to Kay. Anna went to get Kay.

"Hi, Kay," Roy said softly and sweetly. "I'm so sorry that I'm not there. When I got home this evening, I found my young brother waiting for me. He has some problems that he needs help with. I've been talking with him and just realized that it was getting late. I'm so sorry about making you wait for me. I would never have done that on purpose."

Kay wasn't upset. She had been getting a little worried about him, though. "That's okay, Roy. I knew that something must have come up. I understand. You should help your brother tonight. I don't think that I've ever met him. What is his name?"

"He's seventeen and a senior at Litton High School. His name is John. Would you like to meet him? I was just thinking of taking him somewhere to get some supper. I don't think that he has eaten anything at all today. He was pretty upset about something, but I think that he's feeling better now after we talked. Would you like for us to pick you up and get something at the Star Cafe? John loves their pizza burgers as much as I do. I know that you like them, too." Roy hoped that he would still get to see her for a little while tonight.

"I've already had supper tonight, but I guess that I would enjoy a soft drink. I'd like to meet him. Why don't I drive and meet you guys there? That way you can just take him home after we are done at the cafe. I don't mind driving at all. How about I meet you guys there at eight o'clock? I'm pretty sure that they stay open until ten-thirty." Kay was already thinking ahead to what she wanted to wear. It was kind of exciting to meet Roy's brother.

Kay told her mom what had happened and where she was going. Her mom told her to be careful and have fun. Roy's car was already in the Star Cafe parking lot when Kay drove up. She parked next to it and looked at her dress. It was a soft pink one that she knew looked good with her eyes and hair. Roy had mentioned one time that she looked so pretty in pink.

Roy and John were sitting at the counter in the cafe when Kay went in. It was easy to see that John and Roy were related. They had the same color hair and eyes. Something about their faces was the same, too.

Kay smiled sweetly at both and held out her hand to John. "Hi, John, I'm Kay. When Roy called to tell me that you were visiting,

I thought that it would be nice to meet you." She sat down on the stool next to Roy.

Roy looked at her with admiration in his eyes. He thought that she looked beautiful in her pink dress, and he wished that he could give her a kiss. However, they were in public, and that would never do.

"Thanks for meeting us here, Kay. May I buy you a soft drink or some dessert? Or, if you can manage it, a pizza burger?" Roy asked her quietly.

"I'll just have a Pepsi, Roy. Thanks." Kay was a little shy with him. So far, they had only hung out as a couple at her house.

John just stared at her, struck by her beauty. He could see why Roy had a crush on her for so many years. And now they were dating. His admiration for his older brother raised a few notches. If Roy could date someone as sweet and beautiful as Kayleen Harris, he might have a chance with the girl of his dreams.

The three ate and drank while they talked about general things. John told them what Litton High School was like now. So many things had changed, while so many other things stayed the same year after year.

They were chuckling about John's description of the lunchroom during the senior's lunchtime. The associate principal still watched the class like a hawk during lunch. Over the years, he had often made the statement, "There will be no shenanigans in the lunchroom while I'm on duty."

John had his voice down pat. It was hilarious, because John even perfected Mr. Fox's mannerisms, down to the way he would put one foot up on a chair and hook his thumb under his belt as he leaned in to make a point—which he seemed to do frequently.

Kay thought that John was a sweet boy. He started to warm up to her the longer they talked. They talked until the cafe owner called out that they were closing. It was 10:30 pm. Kay didn't have to get up early the next day, but Roy had to be at work by 7:30 am.

Roy had quickly called his mom before they headed out to the Star Cafe and told her that John would be staying the night. He would drive John to school in the morning. Roy told her not to worry about anything—everything was fine. He would pick up John after school tomorrow and bring him home. Roy said that he wanted to talk with the family about something. With that, his mom had to be satisfied. She was worried, but Roy had sounded very calm.

Roy and John walked Kay to her car. John commented on what a sweet car she had. Kay just smiled and agreed. John wanted to give Roy and Kay a quiet moment together, so he said that he wanted to take a quick walk down the sidewalk to work off some of his supper.

He said that he would be back in ten minutes. He felt that ten minutes was long enough for Roy to say goodbye to Kay. Since he had never been on a date, he didn't know that a couple often took much more time than ten minutes to kiss and hug each other goodbye.

Roy was grateful for the ten minutes that John gave him. He looked at Kay with love and tenderness. He was very grateful that she hadn't been upset tonight. She had even driven out to see John and him.

"Thank you, Kay. It was sweet of you to come out and meet John. I could tell that he liked you. He doesn't say much to anyone, even the family." Roy kissed the hand that he held. "You look so beautiful in that pink dress, Kay. I want to kiss you so much. Are you okay with that? It's kind of public right here." He glanced around. There was no one else around them.

Kay smiled sweetly at him. "Thank you for the compliment, Roy. I'm glad that I had the chance to meet John. He seems like a nice boy."

She moved closer to him and lifted her face for his kiss. She was showing him with actions, not words, that she liked him and would welcome his kiss. Roy grinned and swept her into his arms and gave her a long kiss. They stood there, just kissing in the parking lot. They had no idea of the time—John came back in ten minutes, looked at them for a few seconds, and turned his back toward them out of respect for their privacy.

He leaned on Roy's car, looking up at the night sky until Roy was ready to go. It was an eye-opener for John. He had never thought of Roy as being a romantic man, but here he was, kissing the most beautiful girl that John had ever seen. She must be enjoying it because her arms were around Roy's neck.

Roy felt John's presence and drew back from Kay. *Wow!* he thought. *That was some kiss.* Kay had definitely kissed him back and even had her arms around his neck. Maybe she liked him more than he had even hoped. He would have to see how things went the next few times that he saw her. He gave her a quick kiss on her forehead and helped her into her car. He waved at her as she drove away.

Roy turned to look at John. His younger brother had a huge smile on his face. "Wow, Roy, you two would have steamed up the windows if you would have been in your car! You both really do like each other, don't you?"

Roy opened the car door for John, looked at him seriously, and said, "I love Kay. I've been in love with her for years. I intend to marry her someday. She doesn't know it yet, but now that you do, 'Mum's the word', okay? I'm not ready to tell Mom and Dad, yet. We'll probably date for a few more months, and then I'd like to tell her before Christmas. If she loves me, too, I'd like to get engaged at Christmas and maybe get married next year sometime. Now don't say a word to anyone about this. It will be our little secret."

John was glad that he had taken a chance and gone to see Roy. He now felt that Roy would help him and their family. John knew that Tom and his father were not interested in talking about anything that didn't have to do with the farm. That was one of the reasons why John never talked with anyone. He hadn't felt comfortable sharing his innermost thoughts and feelings with them. As a result, he had always thought that there was something wrong with him. He seemed to feel things more deeply than everyone else in his family.

Occasionally, John would entertain the thought that Roy would understand. However, Roy had always been so quiet himself that John didn't have the gumption to ask him about anything. He remembered that Roy talked with him a year or so ago and made him promise to seek him out if he needed help. That's why John decided to trust Roy on this recent visit.

John was excited about the idea of working out with Roy and getting in shape. Whenever he tried to eat less at home, his mom or his dad would ask if he was sick or something like that. When he mumbled that he felt fine, they just told him to eat up.

He really hoped that Roy would help him talk to them. He wanted to see his dad and Tom be more fit, too. They both worked hard and long hours. It couldn't be good for them to carry all that extra weight around. Add in the stress of farming, and it was not a good equation.

He knew that it was not good for him either. Heck, he was only seventeen, but he didn't want to be heavy his whole life. Besides, he hoped to ask Caroline to one of the dances at school one of these days.

When they got back to Roy's apartment, they talked for another half hour about weightlifting. Roy explained that they should really work out in a gym, where there were trained people to guide them. He told John that he would be willing to pay for their memberships if John wanted to work out with him a few times a week.

Roy said that there was a health club on the edge of town, only about ten miles from the farm. If John could get Dad's permission to drive into Litton a few evenings a week, Roy would meet him there and work out with him.

Roy laughed and said that he wouldn't mind bulking up a little. He wanted to carry Kay across the threshold on their wedding day. They both laughed about that, but Roy was secretly thinking about doing that very thing. If things went well for them, he might be able to marry Kay as soon as next year.

Roy apologized to John about having to sleep on the couch. John said not to worry. He would rather sleep on the floor in the living room. With the carpet and a few quilts, he would be more comfortable than trying to curl up on the couch.

They set their alarms for early the next morning and said goodnight. After breakfast, Roy had to drive John across town to school and still get to work by 7:30 am. Both were tired after their long day and fell asleep as soon as their heads touched their pillows.

The next morning went off without a hitch. Roy was in his chair at work by 7:25 am. He grinned when he remembered that John had given him a self-conscious hug before they got in the car. He didn't remember ever hugging John before. John had always been too standoffish with his family and had not wanted to hug them. *Well, maybe I hugged John when he was very little,* Roy thought.

Over the years, Roy arrived at the conclusion that he, himself, was a hugger. It was such a good way to convey to someone that you cared about them and their feelings. Part of that was due to his relationship with his grandmother. The other person he hugged a lot was his mom. Of course, he now loved hugging Kay. She felt exactly right in his arms.

He remembered to call Kay and tell her that he would be taking John home tonight. He probably wouldn't be back in town until quite late. He hoped that he would have the chance to see her tomorrow, though.

Kay thought about Roy and John. She had seen how caring Roy was with his younger brother. Being an only child, she could only imagine the bond between siblings. Most of her friends groaned about their siblings. They said that they often wished to be an only child like Kay. Kay had always thought that it would be kind of special to have a brother or sister to talk to and do things with—someone you could intrinsically trust. Someone like her Nana.

She was just glad that she had once had Nana in her life. Nana was like the sister that Kay never had. As she thought about her Nana, Kay smiled. She wondered what Nana would have thought about Roy. Would she like him? Probably. Roy was terrific. He was such a loving and sweet man.

That evening, after taking John out for a healthy supper, Roy took him home. He had all his arguments ready. He wanted to stress to his father that John was almost an adult and should be able to do some of the things that were important to him. If John wanted to get in shape, Roy was all for it. He would take the time to help

John, too. It would eat into his time with Kay or the Playhouse, but John was important to him. They were brothers, after all.

Roy initially had a difficult time bringing it all up. His dad was tired after his long day and didn't look like he was in any mood to hear about how John felt. John sat right next to Roy. He was the one who wanted to change things. It was his responsibility to be there when they talked about it.

"Mom and Dad, John and I want to talk with you about something important. He has been unhappy for a long time and hasn't felt like anyone would understand his feelings. That's why he came to see me yesterday. He was reaching out for someone to help him. Please don't feel hurt that he came to see me. I am so glad he did." Roy turned and looked at John. He gave John an encouraging smile and turned back to look at his parents.

"First, John wants to be called John from now on. He has outgrown the name Johnny. I agree with him. He's almost a man, and John is a good strong man's name. Second, he wants to lose some weight. He doesn't feel healthy or like the way he looks. I would be willing to work out with him at the gym a few nights a week if you would allow him to drive into town to the club. He also would like there to be more healthy food at supper—not so much fatty and salty foods. I certainly agree with that."

Roy turned to look at his mom. He said lovingly, "Mom, you taught me all about how to cook nutritious meals for myself. You said that I should plan to have fruits and vegetables on my plate, along with the meat and potatoes. I know that you believe that. Is there any way that you can cook that way for these guys? It would be healthier for everyone."

Roy's father immediately stood up and roared at him, "You stay out of this, Roy! You haven't lived here in a long time. Who do you think you are—telling us what to eat? Your mother feeds us very well. We never get up from the table still hungry." Thomas' face was bright red with his temper.

Roy was prepared for this. He never thought that his father would go along with all these changes without a fight. His father was a good man, but he was stubborn, too.

"Dad, I'm not asking Mom to change how she cooks. I'm just saying that John would like to eat better. He wants to lose some weight. There's nothing wrong with that. If he doesn't feel good about himself being heavy, why shouldn't he be able to change his diet and get healthier?"

Thomas said, "He works hard enough on the farm. He should be able to lose weight just by the work he does. Why do we all have to change our food just so he can lose weight? Just eat less, boy." Thomas glared at John in frustration.

"Well, will you at least let John drive the truck into town a few nights a week and work out with me?" asked Roy. He knew that some things just took a long time to change. He would back off on the food, but he planned to bring it up other times when he was home. He and his father had a good relationship these days, and he didn't want to ruin it.

Thomas said gruffly, "If it doesn't interfere with his homework or his chores, I guess that he could take the truck to meet you in town. How many days would that be?"

Roy said, "I thought that we could go on Tuesdays and Thursdays, and maybe the occasional Saturday—*after* all the chores are done. I would be happy to do the Saturday afternoon chores with you so that John could get away quicker. I know that working out seems weird to you, but it really worked for me in college. Remember how skinny I used to be? Working out helped me get my muscles and whole body toned. It can do that for John, too. If you ever want to try it, I can get guest memberships for any of you to try it, too."

He looked at everyone there. Tom had been sitting there watching and listening, not saying a word. Roy thought that he might get a call from him later. Tom had called him a few times previously to vent about some things that were bothering him about working with their dad.

Selma sat there, fighting back her tears. Her little Johnny refused to talk with anyone for years about what he was thinking or how he was feeling. While she was happy that he finally went to see Roy, she felt that she had failed him. As much as she wanted to have an open relationship with all her boys and her husband, it had been only Roy that she had gotten to talk with her. She wondered if it was too late to start with Johnny. *No*, she reminded herself, *I must remember to call him John.*

She privately thought for years that it would be a good idea to eat healthier. Whenever she tried to introduce more fruit and vegetables on the table in the past, her husband said some disparaging remarks about them. He seemed happiest when she served him the starch and meat that he liked the best.

She thought that it was not good for him, but his strong forceful voice and personality made her just go along with what he wanted. She was determined to try to help John with his weight. She was a thin woman herself, but she knew that she could help her boy.

Roy looked at his father with love. He knew that once his dad had time to process all of this, he would very likely go along with all the suggestions that Roy made tonight. He looked at John and winked quickly at him. No one else could see it, but he wanted John to know that things would be okay.

He talked with John on the way here about eating better at school, too. If John could have a good healthy breakfast and lunch, he might still start to lose weight. Although, if he knew his mom, he knew that she would find a way to make supper a healthier meal for all of them.

Roy changed the subject and started talking about the farm. He asked his dad if he wanted him to take a week off work in October to help with the harvest. Roy did that last year, and it had really helped his dad. Thomas looked at Roy with fondness and said that he would appreciate that. They made their plans, and the evening ended on a high note.

Selma put a big jar of apple butter in Roy's hands just before he left. She knew that he loved it. No one else in the family cared either way about it. They would eat it if it was on the table, but they never requested it.

Roy kissed her face lovingly. He knew that she listened and really heard every word that he had said tonight. He knew that he could count on her support to help John. He hugged her and told her that he would see her on Saturday.

Tom and John walked him out to his car. Tom nodded at Roy and said he might give him a call one of these days. Roy knew that was code for "expect a call from me soon". He nodded. Then he turned to John and gave him a high five.

John was pleased with how accommodating his dad had been. Like Roy, John knew that his dad was a good man. Thomas just needed a little extra time to work through things. He was a reasonable man. He would eventually come to see that Roy's words made sense.

Roy smiled at them and waved when he drove away. It was too late to call Kay. He wanted to tell her all about his talk with his family. *I'll do that tomorrow,* he thought.

Eight

The next few days were crazy for Kay. Debbie's boyfriend and father helped her move. Debbie wanted the smallest bedroom because she didn't think that she would be in the house very often. Besides working full-time, she spent much of her time at Donny's house with him and his family. She said that she was basically just going to sleep at Kay's house.

The hospital called and interviewed Kay. They were very impressed with her credentials and her work experience. They had a new position that they wanted to offer her. They wanted someone to work thirty hours a week. She would have to cover the lunches for three full-time nurses and transition the night crew into their jobs. That meant that she would be very busy the whole time and work in several different wings of the hospital every day.

Kay was young and healthy, so she said that she would take it. The hours were good—from eleven in the morning until five o'clock in the afternoon. That way she could take care of errands in the morning before she went to work, and she would be home for supper. She had every Saturday and Sunday off, as well.

Kay had a money legacy from her maternal grandmother that ensured that she would never have to have a job in her life, but she was not about to sit around doing nothing. She liked nursing and was happy to take the part-time job. It meant that she didn't have full health insurance, but she was still covered under her parents' policy until she was twenty-six. *By then I will either be married or working full time,* she thought.

Roy came over and explained that John and he were going to work out at the gym on Tuesday and Thursday nights for a while. That might preclude him from acting in further plays. If the director called rehearsals on those nights, Roy would have to miss them. Now that he had promised John that he would help him, Roy was not going to back out. He would just have to give up the plays for a while if the rehearsal times didn't fit in with his new schedule.

Roy hoped that he could still see Kay on the other nights, though. He told her that right after he kissed her deeply. Kay had been in a little daze and had to agree. She didn't want her sweet Roy to stop seeing her. She was willing to share him with his brother.

During the first week in October, Roy took a week off from his job. He spent the entire week at his parents' home. It was strange to sleep in his old room again and be treated like he still lived at home.

He was hot and sweaty at the end of every long day. Roy, his dad, and his brothers would drag themselves into supper, filthy and sweaty. He hated to sit down at the supper table like that, but his mom always told them to sit down and eat while the food was hot. He showered right after he was done eating, though. He was happy to see that there was usually some kind of fruit or vegetable on the table these days. *Oh well, baby steps,* he thought.

Roy noticed that his dad was very gray in the face at the supper table. He was using his inhaler quite a lot, as well. Thomas physically worked very hard for a sixty-one-year-old man. He had inherited the farm from his father when he was in his late twenties. He met Selma when he was thirty-five, and she was twenty-five. They married after a yearlong courtship. Now he was just plain tired out. The farm took all his energy and that of his sons, as well. It wasn't so bad in the winter, but planting and harvesting times were grueling.

Roy missed Kay every day. She had accepted that he would be working hard on the farm during harvesting and wouldn't have the time to call her or go to see her. She said that she would miss him, but she understood. It was okay because she was adjusting to her new job and her roommate, anyway.

Kay made a quick trip to Chicago with her parents to look at the house that her dad liked. They all loved it, so Sterling and Anna decided to buy it. They hired a moving company to move their belongings to their new home. Kay was a big help to them and very supportive.

That had been before she started her new job, so she was available to help them any way she could. While she felt sad that they were leaving, she knew that she could go and see them anytime. She had every weekend off, and it only took seven hours to drive there one way. If she took a Monday or a Friday off, she would have a three-day weekend.

Her father still had some of his business in Litton. He used to go to Chicago every two weeks, but now that he lived there again, he would flip flop that and come out to Litton every two weeks. Anna could come with him any time she liked. Because she was a housewife, she didn't have to ask for time off from another job. Since their new house was so large, Anna hired another housekeeper to help her with all the work. The housekeeper was always willing to stay in the house whenever Sterling and Anna went to Litton.

After the harvest was done on the farm, Roy went back to his job. His supervisor was agreeable to Roy asking for that time off each year. He was from a farming family himself. Roy continued to work out at the health club with John. He was building more muscle, and he noticed that he was stronger than ever before. His polo shirts showed the definition in his upper torso.

Kay had gently slid her hands along his torso and shyly told him that she liked it. Roy had been very pleased and almost picked her up to show his strength. No, he would wait for the right moment, possibly their wedding day. He planned to carry her over the threshold of their home.

Roy grinned to himself every time he thought about being married to Kay. He found that he loved her more with each passing day. She was so emotionally strong and understood him as well as her friends and parents. Not only was she lovely to look at, but she was also just as lovely inside, too. He adored her. Roy was still taking his time wooing her, and he could tell that she had some deep feelings for him, too.

Their kissing had progressed nicely, and now he had to stop himself from getting too passionate. Although he was ready to ask her to marry him, he didn't want to frighten her in any way. Already a responsible young man, he felt that he would be a good husband.

* * *

While at work one day in late October, Roy got an urgent call from Tom. Their father had a heart attack and was rushed to Litton Hospital that afternoon. Selma had gone with him in the ambulance. Tom was just about to pick John up from school. They would meet Roy at the hospital.

Roy quickly talked to his supervisor, who gave him his blessing to leave. Roy rushed to the hospital and into the waiting room. He saw his mom sitting there alone, too shocked to even cry. He crouched in front of her and gave her a gentle hug.

"Mom, can you tell me what happened?" Roy asked her, with his arms still around her thin shaking body.

Selma turned to look at him blankly. It took her a full minute to pull herself together enough to answer him. "The doctors said that it was a massive heart attack. He is in critical condition."

Now the tears started to fall, thick and fast. "Oh, Roy, he looked so ill. He couldn't catch his breath at all. His eyes looked full of pain. I'll never forget how he looked at me." She cried in Roy's arms for a long time. He just held her tightly. He knew that she would feel better after she had cried away some of her pain.

Selma accepted his hanky and blew her nose. "I noticed that your dad seemed exhausted at lunch. He hardly ate anything. His skin was so gray. Since there wasn't that much to do today, I suggested that he sit in the living room and just relax for a few minutes. I was really shocked when he did that. I was in the kitchen doing the dishes when I heard him cry out. It was loud and like a scream. I ran in there, and he stopped yelling, but just looked at me with eyes filled with pain. I ran out to the shed to get Tom. We called for the ambulance to come. By the time they got there, your dad was struggling to breathe. The men in the ambulance said that he was having a heart attack. They took me with them because Tom had to go and get John. Once we got here, they took him straight to the ICU. After about fifteen minutes, a doctor came to talk to me. He told me that Thomas had had a massive heart attack and was in critical condition. They were not sure if he would survive the night."

Selma started crying again at that point. Roy pulled a chair up next to her and sat down in it. He had his arm around her shoulder and was holding her hand when John and Tom rushed in.

Roy quietly updated his brothers. Both hugged Selma and sat down in some chairs next to her. The Hillmans didn't talk very much—they were just there for each other.

Kay was working at the hospital when the ambulance brought Thomas in. It was not her ward, but she heard about Thomas, anyway. As soon as she had a free minute, she went to see Roy. She was still in her uniform, and she looked very pretty and professional.

Roy was surprised to see Kay, but very grateful, as well. She quietly came up to him and Selma. She laid a gentle hand on Selma's arm. Selma looked up to see who had touched her. She recognized Kay from her photographs and from knowing the family for six years. She was surprised to see the concern on this beautiful young woman's face. She looked at Roy and Tom and John. She saw the welcome in John and Roy's faces.

Kay looked at John and said a quick hello. He smiled wanly at her. Roy smiled a little more warmly at her, but his face was still full of concern and fear. Kay said quietly, "Mrs. Hillman, I heard about your husband. The doctors are with him right now and doing everything they can for him. Can I get you anything? A coffee or a cool drink?" Then she looked back at Roy and asked, "Can I get any of you men a drink? You might feel better with a hot cup of coffee."

Roy looked at his mom and his brothers and quietly said, "Thank you, Kay. If you could bring us some hot coffee, we would appreciate it. If you need a hand with it, I'll come with you." He really needed a hug from Kay just then. She could sense that so she said, "Oh, Roy, that would be helpful. I think that I can carry two cups if you'll get the other two cups. Follow me."

She smiled gently at the others and then turned to lead Roy out of the room. As soon as they were around the corner and out of sight of the waiting room, Roy took her in his arms. She went willingly and held him tightly around the waist. She wanted to give him some comfort. He buried his face in her neck, and they just stood like that for a few minutes. She felt a few hot tears on her neck and just hugged Roy even more tightly. She didn't mind if he shed some tears. After all, his father was fighting for his life. Roy might lose his dad tonight.

Roy got himself under control and looked at Kay's face. She didn't know it, but she had the most loving look on her face. He couldn't believe it. *Kay loves me. She really loves me,* he thought. It was the most amazing miracle that could have happened to him. He hoped that he was not going to gain her love but still lose his father on the same night.

Roy squeezed her tightly and bent down to gently kiss her cheek. He wanted to kiss her properly, but with the way he was feeling right now, he might not be able to stop. They were going to have to have a talk—and soon. But not tonight. He needed to be there for his family.

"Thank you for that, Kay. You don't know how much better you made me feel. Let's get those cups of coffee for my family. As soon as I can, I'll call you and see when I can drop by, okay?" He kissed her lightly on her lips and was gratified when she quickly pressed her lips back on his. He hugged her one more time and then let her go. He quickly swiped at his eyes to make sure that his tears were gone before they went back into the waiting room to hand out the coffee.

Selma drank her coffee slowly and looked at her sons. They were all such wonderful young men. They were a tower of strength for her right now. Her gaze fell onto Roy. She could see the remnants of tears in his eyes. She didn't remember seeing him cry. Did he cry when he left with Kay? They had been gone for quite a while, just getting coffee.

"Roy, it was nice to see Kay Harris. I didn't know that she worked here. You two seemed close. And she seemed to know John, too." She looked him straight in the eyes. *He has never lied to me,* she thought. He was an honest young man.

Roy looked at her and decided to tell all of them his secret. After all, if Kay loved him, he would be asking her to marry him as soon as he could.

"Yes, Mom. We are close. I've been seeing her ever since she came back to Litton. She was in the play with me. We've been dating for the last two months. John met her the night he came to Litton to see me. I love her, Mom. I've always loved Kay. I intend to marry her. I've just been waiting for her to love me back. Tonight, I think I saw love on her face for me. I plan to go and see her tomorrow or the next day to find out if she does love me. If so, I want to propose to her. I would love to get married sometime next year." Roy was glad to have finally told her. They were close, and he didn't like keeping secrets from her.

Selma smiled for the first time in many hours. She was very happy for Roy. She had known that he had feelings for Kay Harris for many years. She hoped with all her heart that Kay loved him back. She would welcome such a sweet and lovely young woman into her family.

Tom stood up and hugged Roy tightly. "Congratulations, Roy. She certainly is a very beautiful girl. If she loves you back, you are one lucky guy. Why did you keep all this such a secret?"

Roy said he wasn't sure. He guessed that it was because he was so unsure of Kay's feelings for him. He had known that he loved her for so long, but he didn't know that she liked him until the night that the play was over. He just wanted to take things slow with her and give her time to fall in love with him, too. He explained all of that to his family. They understood.

They sat up all night, keeping vigil. The doctors came out a few times and updated them on Thomas' progress. He had survived the night. The next few days would be touch and go. He was not out of the woods yet. The doctors advised that they should go home and get some sleep, but none of them wanted to do that.

While they sat there, they came together as a family. Selma finally got John and Tom to talk about their feelings. Tom was concerned that he wouldn't be able to keep the farm going if Thomas was unable to work on it anymore. He loved the farm but knew that he would need more help if he was going to keep it running.

John said that he loved the farm, too. He knew that the farm would go to Tom, as the eldest son. Where did that leave John? He didn't want to live the rest of his life in Tom's house. What if Tom got married? What if John wanted to get married someday?

Selma was amazed at the things that her sons finally talked about. They had obviously been thinking about these things for a long time. It had taken their father's heart attack to finally loosen their voices. They talked about the issues that Tom and John brought up.

Roy said that he would be willing to help occasionally, but he had his own job to think about. He also had Kay to think about, too.

None of them wanted Roy to give up anything that he had going in his life. He had chosen a different path, and they were all okay with that.

Tom finally looked at John and said, "What do you think about being my partner on the farm after you graduate? I know that I'll need some help. You're the best worker that I could ever get. You know everything about the farm. Maybe we could share the property equally. There is enough room to build another house on the property. We could be partners and share everything right down the middle."

John looked astounded and said, "Do you mean that you would share everything, 50-50? If Dad leaves you the farm, I don't expect you to do that, Tom. I'm not sure how to work things out, but I never expected that you would share it equally with me."

Tom smiled widely at his young brother. "I think that would work out well. If I want to get married, I could take some time off and know that you were looking after the farm. The same goes for you—although you better not get married before me, boy. It's bad enough that Roy will marry before me. I haven't even met my dolly girl yet."

John looked secretive and happy. "Well, I've met my dolly girl already. I'm going to ask Caroline Humphries out next week. I've been talking with her for a few weeks, and I think that she likes me, too. Roy taught me how to talk with girls."

Tom looked at Roy incredulously. "Roy did? Wow, when did he get to be such an expert?"

Roy told Tom and his mother the story about how he learned how to flirt. After that, talking to girls was easy. He looked at John and grinned. John hadn't told him that he was ready to ask Caroline out. John had been working hard and had lost ten pounds already.

He was slimming down, and his muscles were starting to show. If he kept this up, he would be in really good shape by next summer.

In the morning they were all tired and hungry. Thomas' main doctor had come out to talk with all of them. He had been serious when he told them that if Thomas survived this heart attack, he would need to make some drastic changes. He would have to eat better and start an exercise program. He wouldn't be able to work on the farm the way he had, either.

They all soberly thought about everything they heard. The doctor also said that there was a very real chance that Thomas would have a second heart attack if he didn't change his lifestyle. That was the most concerning information of all.

Tom said that it was good that the harvest was done. There would be a lull before they needed to do much more on the farm. By the spring, they might have some other plans in place. Roy called his boss and told him that he needed to have the day off. His boss was understanding and told him to take as much time as he needed.

Selma refused to go home, so Roy went looking for some breakfast for all of them. He found the cafeteria and brought back some coffee, hard-boiled eggs, and fruit. There wasn't a large selection of food to be had that early in the morning. Oh well, it was nutritious, at least.

Roy quietly asked John if he wanted him to call into school and get him excused for the day. Since John was not yet eighteen, it needed to be done by an adult. Roy didn't want to bother his mom about doing that. John nodded, so the two of them walked to the telephone and made the call. Roy had his arm around John's shoulder, and it felt good. They had come together as a family last night.

John quietly thanked Roy. Roy squeezed John's shoulders and let him go. He could tell that John was still not very comfortable hugging people. Roy thought, *Give it time.* Once John found someone to love, he would be wanting to hug her all the time. Roy grinned about that. That reminded him that he wanted to talk with Kay tonight. He hoped that he wouldn't be too tired to visit her.

During the long day, they had periodic visits from Thomas' doctors. Selma was finally allowed to see him for a few seconds. She had to look at him from the window outside his room. It scared her to see Thomas all hooked up to tubes and machines. She wished that she could hold his hands and talk with him.

The doctors told her that if Thomas continued to make progress, Selma would be allowed to sit with him for a few minutes. She was getting quite tired by now, but she didn't want to go home. It was too far away, in case she had to get back here in a hurry.

Roy's apartment was also distant from the hospital, and he only had his one twin-size bed. They couldn't all take a nap on it. Selma remembered that there was an inexpensive, but clean and decent, motel near the hospital. As their mother, she was going to suggest that they all go there and take a nap. She broached this subject to her sons. They all thought that it was a marvelous idea, but they wanted one of them to stay at the hospital, just in case there was news.

Tom stated that he would take the first shift. He said that he was fine and could nap in a waiting room chair while everyone else rested at the motel. In four or five hours, one of the other boys could relieve him. Roy volunteered to do that.

Roy got his mom and John situated in their rooms at the motel. His mom had her own room, but the boys would share the other one. There were two beds in his and John's room, anyway. Roy said goodnight to John, set his alarm for four hours, and immediately went to sleep. When his alarm went off, he took a quick shower and drove himself to the hospital. John and Selma were still sleeping. Tom looked haggard when Roy got there to relieve him, but he reported that there was no news about Thomas.

Roy gave him the key to the motel room and told him to get some sleep. Before Tom left, he brought Roy a sandwich and some coffee from the cafeteria. He planned to take his mom and John out to eat before they came back to relieve Roy in about five hours.

Roy looked down at his clothes. They were the same ones that he had worn yesterday. He thought that he looked horrible, but at least he had showered. He was just sitting there thinking about his dad when Kay walked in. He admired how pretty and fresh she looked. She came over to him and sat down in one of the chairs. She smiled kindly at him and took his hands in hers.

"I asked about your dad, and the doctors said that he was making progress. I'm so happy for you, Roy. I know how much you love your father." Kay's voice was caring and sweet. She looked around the room. "Where is your mom? And your brothers?"

Roy explained about the motel room and taking shifts. He apologized for his dishevelment.

Kay just shook her head and said that she had seen much worse. She didn't care what his clothes looked like, she just cared about Roy. It was fun to see him in the morning, though. He hadn't had the chance to shave, and his chin was covered with bristles. She wanted to touch them, but she thought that Roy might not like that.

Roy saw her looking at his chin. He felt his chin and grinned wryly. "I guess I need a shave, don't I?" He chuckled tiredly.

"Until we know that Dad's going to be fine, we're going to need to stay around here. Meanwhile, I'm going to have to drive home sometime tonight. I must get some more clothes and shave because I can't stay in these same clothes for another day."

He took Kay's soft hands in his. He wanted to tell her that he loved her, but he didn't think it was the right time. He was tired, in a mess, and Kay was at work. If he could just get some sleep tonight, he would try to see her tomorrow evening at her house.

Kay sat with him for fifteen minutes. They just held hands and sat quietly. When she got up to go, she leaned over and kissed him. It was the first real kiss that she had initiated. She pressed her soft lips down on his and kissed him hard. Then she smiled sweetly at him and told him to take care of himself. She waved from the door and then went quickly around the corner.

Roy perked up and felt very alive all at once. *Kay must care about me to kiss me like that,* Roy thought with happiness. He daydreamed about Kay and their happy life together until his family arrived to relieve him. Selma and John looked much better for their long nap. Tom still looked tired, but then so did Roy. The brothers looked at each other and smiled. They were here to get their mother through a tough day. What was tiredness, compared to her comfort?

Thomas continued to make steady progress that day. By that evening, he was markedly better. Selma had been allowed to sit with him for a few minutes. Although she didn't think that he could hear her, she talked quietly to him. First, she told him that she loved him. Then she told him that his sons were all doing well, and they were finally talking together as a family. She told him to hurry up and get better so he could come home to her. She blew him a kiss from the door when the nurse told her that she had to leave. She felt much better after seeing him and talking to him.

She wanted to stay in the motel room, close to the hospital, that night, as well.

Tom told her that he and John would drive back to the farm and get some clean clothes for the three of them. They would bring everything back with them and stay the night with her at the motel. Roy said that he would stay with her at the hospital until they got back. After that, he wanted to go home and get clean clothes for himself.

Tom insisted that they would be okay at the motel and that Roy should go home and stay there. He should get a good night's sleep in his own bed. They would call him if they needed him to come back to the hospital. Roy reluctantly agreed and sat talking quietly with his mom until Tom and John came back an hour or so later.

Roy kissed and hugged his mom before he left to go home. He looked at his two brothers with love and nodded to them. He put his hand on their shoulders as he said goodbye. He knew that his brothers were too uncomfortable to hug him yet, but they would get there eventually. He just knew it in his heart. He promised that he would see them back at the hospital tomorrow morning around eight o'clock.

Roy was very weary by the time he got home that night. He had told Kay earlier that day that he probably wouldn't have the chance to talk with her again that night. She had been fine with that. He fell into bed and slept like a log until his alarm woke him up at six o'clock the next morning. He called in sick to work one last time, showered, shaved, dressed in nicer clothes, and had a good breakfast. He felt so much better than he had yesterday.

No one had called him during the night, so he was positive that his father was doing better. He got to the hospital by eight o'clock. He arrived a few minutes before Tom, John, and his mom walked in.

They all looked much better, too. Tom had shaved, and they were all showered and in clean clothes. Roy grinned at them. They were all ready to face another day.

That whole day, they made plans regarding Thomas' care when he came home from the hospital. The doctors said that Thomas would likely remain in the hospital for a week or more. They would assess his condition every day and let the family know when he could go home.

Even though Roy would have to go back to his job, his boss would allow him to take time off, as needed. John would go back to school, with the knowledge that Tom or Roy would come and get him if need be. Selma would eventually go back to her kitchen and get things ready for Thomas' return to their home.

Tom, John, and Selma were going to stay one more night at the motel. Tomorrow, if Thomas was still progressing, they would check out and go home. Until Thomas was up to having visitors, they would be at home, getting things ready for his homecoming.

Roy planned to go back to his job tomorrow. That afternoon, he delivered a nice deli meal to his family. Then he kissed and hugged his mom, clapped his brothers on the back in a sign of support and love, said his goodbyes, and drove home to his apartment.

Nine

It was still early—only five pm. Roy knew that Kay worked until then and wouldn't be home for a little while yet. He really wanted to go to her and tell her that he loved her. The scare regarding his father had impressed on him that life was a vapor. You shouldn't put off the important things. The doctors had told them tonight that Thomas would probably be fine, provided he changed his lifestyle. If not, he could expect another heart attack.

Roy knew that he wanted his father to be at his wedding. He planned to propose to Kay tonight and beg her to marry him before Christmas. That didn't give her a lot of time to plan a wedding, even if she did say yes. He wanted them to have a white wedding. He could just imagine her in a beautiful white wedding gown and veil walking down the aisle to him. He daydreamed a little about her and then shook himself. He had to be alert and thinking tonight.

Once inside his apartment, he shaved again, just to make sure that his cheeks and chin were nice and smooth. He hoped that Kay would be touching his face while they kissed tonight. He tried out his new aftershave. *Umm, it smells nice*, thought Roy. Then, he put on his best suit.

Roy wanted to come to her tonight with an engagement ring, but he didn't know Kay's ring size. He knew that she had slender fingers, but he didn't want to give her something that she couldn't wear right away. Reasoning that she might like to pick out her own ring, anyway, he decided that he would bring her a bunch of red roses. He looked himself over once more in the mirror and then went to call her.

Kay answered, "Hello," in her sweet voice.

"Hello, Kay. This is Roy. I was wondering if I could come over tonight and talk with you. I've missed sitting on the swing with you. Is Debbie there?" Roy didn't want Kay's roommate coming out of her room and messing up his proposal.

"Hi, Roy. I've missed you, too. No, Debbie is spending the evening with Donny and his parents. They're going out to that good steakhouse for supper. She said that she probably wouldn't be home until about ten or eleven tonight. She has a key, so it's no big deal when she comes in. Why did you ask about her?" Kay had a smile in her voice. She thought that Roy might be wanting to kiss her, and he didn't want Debbie walking in to see them.

"Oh, I just wondered. If it's okay with you, I'll be there in an hour. Do you want to go out to eat, or will you make us a sandwich? I won't have eaten yet when I come over." Roy hoped that she would just make them a sandwich.

"Would you rather go out or eat in? I don't mind either way," Kay asked him.

Roy said, "I want you all to myself, so I'd rather eat in if you don't mind."

Kay chuckled softly. "Okay, Roy, I'll make some supper for us. I hope you won't be disappointed. I'm not a great cook, yet. My mom always made our meals. Now that she moved out, I'm having to learn by myself. I promise that whatever it is, it'll be edible, though."

Roy laughed delightedly. "Oh, Kay, I don't expect anything grand. A sandwich will be fine. I'll see you in about an hour, alright?"

Kay confirmed that she would be ready with a meal.

Before he left his apartment, Roy called Sterling and Anna Harris. He had something to ask them.

Anna answered the phone, and her voice was warm when she realized who she was talking with. Roy asked if Sterling was there. She went to get him. Roy asked her to get on the other extension if she had one. Once both parents were on the line, Roy asked for their permission to marry their daughter.

"I love Kay with all my heart. She is the only woman that I have ever loved or could love. I promise that I will cherish her every day of my life." Roy's love for Kay came through loud and clear.

Sterling thanked Roy for his call, and both he and Anna gave Roy their blessing. Roy said that he planned to ask Kay to marry him later that evening. He promised that someone would call them back either tonight or tomorrow to let them know Kay's response.

Anna smiled because she already knew what her darling Kay would say. She would say yes to Roy because she loved him, too. After a few minutes, Roy thanked them for their time and hung up. *Whew! Now, that's done.* Roy considered that it was almost scarier to ask her parents for their blessing than to ask Kay to be his bride.

As Roy went out to get the roses, he also stopped and bought a bottle of fine champagne. If she said yes, they would have some celebrating to do.

Kay thought about tonight. Roy had just gone through some emotionally packed days. He would probably be feeling tired and maybe a little sad. She wanted to cheer him up, so she decided to wear her most attractive dress for him.

She wished that she was a better cook, but he had said that a sandwich would be fine for supper. He had very likely eaten hospital cafeteria food for a few days, so she didn't want to give him yet another sandwich. An hour didn't leave her much time to plan and make a fancy meal.

She scoured Nana's cookbooks that were in the cupboard. She finally decided on a recipe for a delicious chicken and rice casserole. It was a meal that her mom made quite often because her dad loved it. It could stay hot in the oven for quite a while in case he came home late.

Kay had grown up with a father who didn't keep regular hours. He often had to stay at work longer than he anticipated. Her mom and she would eat their meal and save enough for her dad. He would drag himself home, exhausted. Anna would quietly re-heat his supper, give him a kiss on the top of his head, and set the hot meal down in front of him.

Sterling always looked at Anna with gratitude and love and tucked into the food like he was starving. Kay wondered if Roy liked that kind of casserole. Well, she did, and it was easy to make.

Kay quickly checked her fridge and cupboards and found that she had everything she needed, with just a few modifications. Instead of green beans, she had peas and carrots. *That should be fine,* she thought. She quickly put all the ingredients together and put the casserole into the oven. If Roy arrived exactly on time, the casserole would be done five minutes before he walked in the door. *Now to shower and change,* she thought.

Kay was ready, and the kitchen smelled delicious when she looked at the clock and saw that it was exactly seven o'clock. A second later, she heard Roy's car come up the driveway. It was a cool evening—too cold to sit outside on the porch swing. They would have to sit in the living room tonight if he wanted to talk.

Kay opened the door to Roy, feeling a little shy for some reason. They had spent many evenings together talking, holding hands, and kissing. She looked at her dress. It was a very soft pale pink sweater dress. It hugged her slender curves and looked perfect with her pink and white complexion, dark hair, and bright blue eyes. Kay felt that she looked her best for Roy.

Roy's eager eyes took in Kay's loveliness. She looked soft and pink and very beautiful. He shyly handed her the dozen red roses that he brought with him. They were gorgeous, long-stemmed, and tied with a red velvet ribbon. Kay's eyes widened; she loved red roses, but she didn't want Roy to spend his hard-earned money on them for her. She accepted them with a sweet smile. He had something in a paper bag, too.

Roy breathed deeply. There was a delicious smell coming from the oven. He followed her into the kitchen and quickly put the bag inside the fridge without saying anything. He turned Kay around into his arms and gave her a long kiss. He kept his arms around her and looked down at her with very bright eyes. His smile was beautiful to see.

"Kay, my dear, you look so beautiful! Something smells delicious, besides you." He grinned happily at her. Kay wondered why he looked so very happy right now. Then she thought she knew—his father must be doing so much better.

Kay looked back at him with soft eyes. Her face was loving, even though she didn't know it. Roy's arms tightened just a little bit more around her when he gazed into her eyes. *I wasn't wrong,* he thought. *It really does look as if my darling Kay loves me.* He had dreamed of this night for so long. He just hoped that it would end the way he wanted it to.

"Kay, I really didn't expect a full meal. I would have been fine with a quick sandwich, you know," Roy told her quietly.

Kay smiled at him and said, "I know that, but I thought that you have probably eaten nothing but sandwiches from the hospital cafeteria for a few days. I wanted you to have a home-cooked meal. This casserole is one of my favorites. I hope that you like it, too."

"I'm sure that I will love it. It smells very good. Is it ready to eat, or should we talk for a little while?" Roy really wanted to eat before they talked. Once he proposed to her, he hoped to have a long stretch of time for kissing afterward.

"It's ready to eat. I set the table in the dining room. Is it okay if we eat there? Nana used to make us eat our meals in the dining room. We could only eat our breakfast in the kitchen. She said it was sloppy mealtime etiquette, otherwise." Kay smiled when she remembered her Nana saying that. She always had such specific expectations about the way things should be properly done.

"That will be fine. I'll carry the casserole in for you if you'll show me where the hot pads are," Roy volunteered. Together, they brought all the food into the formal dining room.

The antique cherrywood table was long and rectangular, adorned with intricate carvings. The leather upholstery on the seats and backs of the chairs was attractive and comfortable. Roy had never eaten at such a grand table in his life. It just made Kay's delicious meal taste even better.

They mostly talked about Thomas and the hospital while they ate. Roy insisted on helping her clear everything away and do the dishes. When everything was done, he gently steered her toward the living room sofa. There he sat her down. He sat next to her and took her hands in his. He bent and kissed her hands gently. Then he looked back into her face. He was ready to tell her that he loved her.

"Kay, I have been doing a lot of thinking while I sat in that hospital waiting to hear if my father would live or die. The one thing I know for sure is that you should never put off doing the things that are the most important to you. No one knows how much time they have left in this world. I want to tell you something now that I have been waiting to tell you for a long time. I love you, Kay, so very much. I have loved you ever since the day I met you. I thought that it was just a crush, but now I know that there has never been anyone else in this whole world for me except you. I have never loved anyone else, and I never will. I tried to go slow with you because I didn't want to frighten you, but now I must let you know that I adore you. I hope that you love me, too. We have grown close these past few months. I want your happiness more than I want it for myself."

Roy got down on one knee in front of her. Kay looked at him with her beautiful eyes, bright with unshed tears. He kissed her hands again and then said, "My darling Kay, will you marry me? I know that I don't have much money or other things to give you, but I give my heart to you. You have held it in your soft, slender hands for such a long time already. I promise that I will love you and cherish you every day of my life and beyond."

Kay's tears finally fell, and she smiled tremulously. She leaned forward and cupped his face. She pressed the sweetest kiss that he could ever imagine onto his lips.

"Yes, Roy, I will marry you. I have loved you for months now. I was so happy when you told me that you liked me and wanted us to start dating. I wanted to tell you at that time that I already loved you, but I didn't think that you loved me yet. I have been patiently waiting for you to fall in love with me. But all along, you already did. My Nana told me that if we were supposed to be together, we would be. Oh, Roy, I'm so happy. I love you so much." Kay's beautiful face was exquisite with her tenderness and love for him.

Roy felt his heart almost burst with happiness and love for Kay. She was everything to him. He would cherish and adore her every day of his life from now on.

Roy got to his feet and gently pulled her to her feet. His arms went around her, and he held her with all the love and tenderness that he felt in his heart. Then he bent and gave her the most beautiful kiss that he had ever given her. Kay's arms came around his neck, and she gave herself up to his glorious kiss. They stood, locked in that kiss for a long, long time. Tears were falling from Kay's eyes when Roy finally released her. She smiled shakily at him and just said softly, "I'm so happy."

Roy tenderly kissed the tears from her face and then briefly touched his lips to her eyelids. She was even more beautiful with her eyes crying because of his love. He sat her back down on the sofa and took her hands in his again. "We need to talk about the wedding, my darling Kay. I know it is very quick, but I would like for us to marry before Christmas. My father's doctors said that he will likely be okay for a while, but he could have a second heart attack at any time if he is not careful enough. I want him to be at our wedding. I just don't know if he'll still be with us next year.

After all, it was a massive heart attack. I know that it is so much to ask, but would you consider marrying me in two months? You could pick the actual date in December." Roy's look was anxious and very hopeful.

"Let me think about that for a few minutes, Roy. I'm not sure that I can get married that quickly." She didn't want to be rushed, even though she understood Roy's reason for requesting a December wedding date.

Roy nodded and said, "Of course, my love. I brought some champagne, just in case we had something to celebrate. I'll go and get it ready for us. That will give you a few minutes to think about everything while I'm in the kitchen. Is that okay?" Roy kissed her forehead gently.

Kay nodded, and Roy took himself off to the kitchen to get their champagne. He planned to take his time so that she had five or ten minutes to consider his request.

Kay knew that her parents would expect her to have at least a six-month engagement in order to have enough time to pull together the big wedding that they desired for her. It would be fun to take her time and plan everything just so. But on the other hand, was all that necessary? She loved Roy, and he loved her—surely that was the only thing that mattered. Maybe they should just have a quiet wedding, with just family.

She had always dreamed of her wedding day. There would be hundreds of guests and five or six bridesmaids. She would glide down the aisle in her mother's beautiful wedding gown. Well, other than the hundreds of guests and five bridesmaids, she could still do the rest of those things.

She was ready to be married to Roy. She had felt that for a few months already. What if she asked Roy to wait until next year to get married and Thomas died before they got married? Would Roy be angry and blame her because his father couldn't be at the wedding? She didn't want that to happen. *It is all such a mess,* she thought.

Kay decided to ask Roy to let her think about it until she talked with her parents. She wanted at least a day to weigh all the pros and cons. She planned to tell him that until she watched him come into the room. He was carefully holding the tray that held their champagne glasses. His face was flushed, but he was smiling very sweetly at her. He looked confident, strong, and patient. She knew that he would help her with anything that she asked him to do. His whole being showed how ready he was to marry her.

Before she could say anything else, she heard herself say, "Darling Roy, of course I will marry you in December. We'll have to make our plans quickly, but there is no reason why we can't pull off a wedding in two months. I want your father to be there at our wedding, too."

Roy set the tray down on the table and took her in his arms. He hugged her tightly and pressed his face into her neck. His words were quiet, but so sincere. "I can't believe that you will marry me in December, my love. I thought that I would have to wait for you until June or July next year. I'm so overcome with gratitude and love that I can barely believe it. Thank you so much, my darling Kay. This means the world to me. If I could, I would marry you this very instant. I love you so much."

He kissed her neck and then kissed her lips. They held each other, just trembling from all the emotion they were both feeling. Finally, Roy looked at Kay and gave her the glass with the champagne bubbling cheerfully. He took the other glass for himself and raised it in front of her. "This toast is for you, Kay. You are the most beautiful woman in the world—inside and out. I am humbled to be your fiancé." She smiled and clinked her glass with his. They both drank some champagne and then sat back down. There was much to discuss that night.

They were still talking about their wedding plans when Debbie got there. With the remaining champagne, they drank another toast with her. It was only a few minutes after ten o'clock, so Roy and Kay decided to call her parents. He told her earlier that he had asked their permission to marry her. Kay laughed delightedly when he told her that. Roy was such a romantic young man. He was so traditional, and she loved it. She imagined that he would write love poems for her on her birthday and for their anniversaries. She couldn't wait to begin her life with him.

Kay's parents were very happy for the newly engaged couple, but they were disappointed that Kay wouldn't have a long engagement and all the trimmings that they wanted her to have. Sterling and Anna became very quiet when Kay explained about Roy's father.

Kay very eloquently said, "The only thing that really matters is that Roy and I love each other and want to marry. Everything else is just fluff. I would marry Roy tomorrow if I could. Don't you see, Mom and Dad, that all the rest of the trimmings are just for show? It doesn't make any difference to the fact that we are getting married and want to be together forever."

Anna quietly cried when she heard her darling Kay put forward her reasons for wanting a shorter engagement. She had to agree that the fact that Roy and Kay loved each other and had pledged themselves together was enough. Anna promised that she would come to Litton with Sterling in a week or so and help Kay plan the wedding. Kay was happy to put her parents up in her house for as long as they wanted to stay. After talking for almost an hour, they finally hung up.

Roy wanted to tell his mom and brothers their good news right away in the morning. Kay didn't have to be at work until eleven, so they had plenty of time. Roy would ask for a few hours off in the morning. His boss had always been very accommodating.

Roy felt so close to Kay right now that he didn't want to leave and go home. He could have sat on the sofa and cuddled and kissed her all night, but they were both tired. He tenderly kissed her goodnight and wished his lovely Kay a sweet night's sleep. He would come over at eight o'clock in the morning to take her to see his family. It was bound to be another emotional scene.

Ten

The next day was as emotional as Roy thought it would be. His mom cried all over him—she was just so happy. Her emotions were already so heightened because of Thomas' illness. Tom hugged both Roy and Kay. It made Roy feel very close to his older brother. They would have to wait to tell John until this afternoon when he got home from school.

Roy told Kay that he had wanted to buy her an engagement ring and give it to her when he proposed but didn't know what size ring she needed. He promised to take her out to buy the ring whenever she wanted to do that. Because it was Friday, they would both have tomorrow and Sunday off to do some more planning.

Roy took her back to her house so she could get ready for work and then went back to his own job. He told his boss and the other people in his office and was heartily congratulated. He said that he really didn't have anything else to say because he and Kay had not yet had time to plan the wedding.

Since Roy didn't have to go to his parents' farm and help with the chores on Saturday, he could devote his whole day to Kay. He pulled into her driveway at nine o'clock that morning and looked around at the house and yard. Kay had already told him last night that she would love it if they could live there for at least a few years.

Because they would have no mortgage to pay, they would both be able to save quite a lot of their salaries. Kay stated that she wanted to keep working at the hospital until they started having babies. They smilingly told each other that they would like at least two or three children, some of each. They found that they agreed on so many of the important things. *It was a very good sign*, they both thought.

Roy liked the old house. It really seemed like a family home—full of quaint little nooks and crannies. He already loved that porch swing. He had wooed his Kay on that for a few months. He could picture them, rocking their babies to sleep, or just cuddling up on it and swinging slowly on it when the weather was fine.

It was a cold day, and Roy looked down at his worn corduroy pants and old sweater. Besides his suits for work and his new summer clothes, he didn't have much else to wear. His winter clothes were old and shabby. Kay was always dressed so beautifully; Roy didn't want her to be ashamed of him.

Well, he hadn't had much time lately to go shopping for new clothes. *Maybe Kay would enjoy shopping with me,* he thought. She had classic good taste and could show him what would look good on him. He fleetingly remembered Alicia, that salesclerk, who had given him her phone number. He had long ago thrown that slip of paper away. Now maybe Kay would flirt with him while she told him which colors looked best on him. Roy grinned widely at that.

Kay was wearing a pretty outfit of velvety deep burgundy corduroy pants and a creamy soft white sweater. Her black hair was loose, and she had a pink flush on her face. *She looks so lovely,* Roy thought.

Roy handed her a perfect single red rose and kissed her soundly. Her flush deepened to a darker pink and her eyes sparkled when he finally let her go. She gently put the rose with the dozen from two nights ago and proclaimed that she was ready to go. At the last minute, she grabbed her lightweight winter coat and leather gloves.

The first place they went was to the jewelry store. Roy had transferred half of his savings to his checking account this morning. He was willing to spend all of it on whatever ring his beautiful Kay wanted. He didn't really think that they would use it all, but he wanted to be prepared. He had saved about ten thousand dollars, and he didn't think that a diamond ring would be more than five thousand dollars. He wanted to buy the one that Kay loved. It would be on her slender finger for seventy years or more, he hoped.

Kay slid her eyes to Roy's outfit. It was shabby. He still looked very handsome to her, but she wondered if she could persuade him to buy a few new things. They were bound to go out and about, and she didn't want him to feel self-conscious. She wondered how she could broach that topic without hurting his pride or his feelings. The clothes he was wearing right now would be perfect for a quiet evening at home, though. If he liked them, he should keep them to wear when they relaxed at home.

Roy saw her glance at his clothes and the conflicted look on Kay's face. He could almost read her thoughts. He nodded slightly to himself. It seemed that Kay was also in favor of Roy buying some new winter clothes. Good—she would probably love to help him with that. They could do that after they bought the rings. He wanted to wear a wedding ring, too. He wanted everyone to see that he was married to his lovely Kay.

They took a long time picking out the rings. Roy told her that she was to buy the ring that she loved; he could afford to buy her whatever she wanted. Kay realized that Roy probably dug deeply into his savings to buy it. She could tell that he wanted her to have the best quality and the prettiest ring that was available to them. Since she had long slender fingers, she didn't want a huge gaudy diamond ring. She thought that a smaller diamond solitaire or cluster ring would look the best on her finger.

She tried several different styles on her finger, and when she realized that she went back to one particular ring three times, she decided that it was the one. It was one that Roy had picked out and silently handed to her, so she knew that he liked it, too. It was a classically simple, beautiful solitaire diamond ring, a third of a carat, mounted in 14 Karat gold. It would look perfect next to a plain gold wedding band.

She tried it on once again and admired its brilliance and perfection. She shyly handed it to Roy and told him that this was the ring she wanted. He took the ring and held her hand for a second, smiling down into her eyes. He was happy with her choice, too.

While Kay had been trying on various engagement rings, Roy had been looking at gold wedding bands. He had seen the one he liked for himself. It was just a plain brushed gold band. He had tried it on, and it felt good. It wasn't too clunky or uncomfortable. He felt that he could easily wear it for the next seventy or more years, too.

He showed her the wedding band that he liked and told her to pick out one for herself. She found a simple gold band that went beautifully with the engagement ring. They held hands while he got out his checkbook and paid for them. All three rings cost quite a bit less than he had been prepared to spend. He was grateful that he still had some money in his account. Now he could justify spending some of that money on new winter clothes.

When they got out to his car, Roy turned to Kay and held out his hand for her left hand. He slid her engagement ring onto her hand and then kissed it. He leaned in close to her and asked again, "My darling Kay, will you marry me?"

Kay smiled at him and reached up to kiss him on his mouth. They kissed in the parking lot for a few minutes until she broke their kiss and said breathlessly, "Yes, darling Roy. I will marry you. Thank you for my beautiful ring. I just love it."

They smiled sweetly at each other before Roy ushered her into his car. He had the two wedding bands in a small bag in his pants pocket. He didn't want to keep them in there if he was going to try on some new pants later. He would have to ask Kay if she could keep them safe in her purse while he tried on new clothes.

"I saw you looking at my old clothes, Kay. You can probably tell that I want to buy some new ones. Would you go shopping with me and help me buy several new sets of winter clothes? I really don't know what looks best on me, but you have such good taste that I hoped that you would help me." Roy looked at Kay with a smile.

Kay said, "Oh, I thought that your summer outfits were nice. They fit you well and were the perfect colors for you."

Roy had to come clean about that. He laughed and said wryly. "Well, my mom bought and gave me the first outfit. She told me that I needed to start caring more about how I dressed. I called her and asked her where she bought them, so I went to the same store to look for a few more sets. I must admit that I didn't know what I was doing, so a very nice salesclerk helped me. That was right after you and Martie taught me how to flirt. I tried flirting with the salesclerk, and it worked. She gave me her number and told me to call her."

Kay laughed. "What? Martie and I taught you how to flirt? When was that?"

"Remember that first time that you, Martie, your mom, and I went to the Dairy Queen after play practice? You and Martie were obviously flirting with me. I listened to how you flirted and then tried it myself. I practiced flirting with your mom that night. She seemed to respond to it, so I tried it the next evening on the salesclerk. I even told my brother, John, how to do it. It was fun. I wish that I would have known how to flirt a long time ago. Then maybe things would have been different for me. Maybe I wouldn't have been so lonely." Roy looked a little sad for a minute.

Kay hugged him and said softly, "I'm sorry that you were lonely, Roy. But selfishly, I am happy, too. If you would have known how to flirt a long time ago, you might have fallen in love with some other girl, and I would never have gotten to know you and fallen in love with you myself. You were so perfect when we met again in June. I wouldn't have wanted you to be any other way. I don't know if I could have fallen in love with a hip, flirty Roy." She reached over and gave him a quick hard kiss on the mouth.

Roy loved the idea that Kay was confident enough to initiate some kisses. He smiled at her and then said thoughtfully, "I guess that I had to go through what I did to become the man I am now. I'm so happy that you fell in love with me the way I am. Hopefully, you know that I'm essentially a quiet man. I love your spark and personality, but that is not who I am. I don't think that I could be a big flirt; I would only want to flirt with you, anyway. I don't need anyone else to admire me—only you, my sweet Kay."

Kay smiled back at him and said softly, "I would like it if you flirted with me sometimes. It would be kind of fun for us. But mostly, I like your quietness. You, my darling Roy, are deep. I imagine that your heart and soul are filled with romantic thoughts. I can't wait to see them. You are exactly right for me. Please don't ever change." With that, she gave him another quick kiss and sat back in her seat. Then she thought of something.

"What ever happened with that salesclerk?" Kay asked in a slightly amused voice. As far as she knew, Roy hadn't gone out with anyone else when he had been rehearsing for the play.

"Oh, I threw her number away a long time ago—a week after she gave it to me. I knew that I would never want to date anyone else but you." He smiled sweetly at her. After one more sweet kiss, Kay sat back and said, "Let's go to the mall. I know the perfect store to find some new clothes for you. Do you have a list of what you want, or should we wing it?"

Roy laughed shortly and said, "Let's wing it. I don't really know what I need. I'm hoping that my future wife will help me." With that, he gave Kay an impish grin.

Kay grinned back and suggested a store, giving Roy directions. They spent the next hour getting a fashionable and warm bunch of new clothes for Roy. She persuaded him to buy a few nice pairs of corduroy pants because they were in style and warm. Minnesota had some very cold winters. She said that he needed a few nice pairs of dress pants that he could wear when he didn't want to wear his suits. Then he needed a few sweaters and other long-sleeved shirts to wear with the new pants.

Roy had not bought so many clothes in a long time. He was astounded at how much money he was spending, but he rationalized that these new clothes would last him for a long time. Also, he would soon be a successful young married man, and he should look the part. They took all his new clothes out to the car.

Roy brought Kay back into the mall and led her to a jewelry store. It was a small store, but he had seen some pretty earrings in the window the last time that he walked past it. She looked at him, quizzically.

Roy said happily, "You just helped me buy a bunch of new clothes. Now I want to buy you a pretty necklace or earrings. I just want to buy my beautiful fiancée a gift."

Kay protested a bit, but Roy took her hand and led her into the store, anyway. Roy described for the salesclerk a pair of delicate earrings that he had seen in the window a month ago. He thought at the time that they would be so pretty on Kay. He noticed that she had pierced ears and that she usually wore dangly earrings. He usually saw her wearing tops and sweaters in soft pastel colors. They all went so well with her complexion, her eyes, and hair color.

The earrings were a clear lavender color—probably man-made amethysts. The gems were tear-shaped and hanging from a string of gold, inset with tiny crystals. Because he had also seen the price in the window, he knew that they were likely cubic zirconia and man-made amethysts, but they had been so pretty.

The salesclerk came back with the earrings on a piece of white velvet. Kay loved them. She knew that Roy understood that they were costume jewelry, not real jewels. She would not have let him buy them if they had been the real thing. They had better things to spend their money on.

Kay was touched that Roy wanted to buy them for her. Since they were only about fifty dollars, she graciously accepted them. In fact, she took off the earrings that she was already wearing and put her new ones on. They went very well with her outfit. She thanked Roy with a big kiss, and they walked out of the store holding hands.

Roy was happy. He could tell that Kay liked the earrings. It was just a little thing, but he wanted to buy them for her ever since he saw them. It was nice to have someone to buy pretty things for. He was going to love being engaged and then married. He thought that if he could afford it, he would surprise Kay with something pretty every once in a while. She deserved every pretty thing that she got.

They spent the rest of the morning and afternoon at the farm. Kay fit right in. She was comfortable with them, and they were comfortable with her. She very gently teased John and was secretly delighted when he flirted shyly with her. In a quiet corner, he told her about Caroline. Kay encouraged him to just be his regular sweet and friendly self with her. He hadn't yet asked her on a date but wanted to ask her to go to the Christmas dance with him.

Roy told his mom about his new clothes, and she insisted that he bring them in and try them on. He was sorry then that he had mentioned it. Against his objections and reluctance, the two women ganged up on him and insisted that he try the new clothes on for them. Kay's eyes were dancing mischievously. She winked at Selma, who smiled widely back at her. Selma knew that if anyone could bring Roy out of his shell, it would be Kay.

Selma very much enjoyed Kay's kind, friendly, and outgoing personality. *Kay is just what we need around here,* Selma thought. Everyone at the Hillman home was so serious and quiet. Kay would breathe some life into all of them. Selma was so happy that Roy had finally done something about his love for Kay. She would be the perfect wife for him.

Roy had to endure a few gibes from Tom when he tried on his new clothes, but he could see that Tom was pretty thoughtful most of the time. He expected that he would get a telephone call one of these days from him about something. John thought that Roy's new clothes were great. He wanted to buy a few new things himself. Now that he was losing some weight, he wanted to dress nicer, too.

Selma smiled at him. He could tell that she read his mind. He had been talking with her a little more and found that she was very practical and never once told him that his hopes or dreams were stupid. She understood him, he was happy to note.

They all discussed the wedding plans that evening. They were very surprised when Roy told them that they were planning to get married in December. When Roy quietly explained that he wanted Thomas to be at the wedding, they all soberly agreed. Thomas was doing better, but still not able to talk with visitors. They planned to visit the hospital each day for a few hours until he was released. The doctors said that Thomas would be fit enough to come home in another week.

Selma had gone through her cupboards and made lists of the kind of food that she would need to buy for Thomas. It would be great for all of them to eat better. John and Tom would also benefit from lean meats and low-salt foods.

John already told her that he wanted to help her in the kitchen. He decided that he was not too young to start learning how to do some of the cooking. Selma was tickled pink by that. That was two of her three sons who would know how to cook. Maybe Tom would want to learn somewhere down the line, too.

Tom was the most like his father. He was a quiet man, who had strong opinions about things. Selma just hoped that he would be okay with the new diet. Thomas' doctors stressed that he could never go back to eating the way he previously had. It was much too fatty, salty, and starchy for him.

Selma was also going to suggest that the family get a membership at the health club that Roy used and that they all go and work out together. Although she was a thin woman, she wouldn't mind getting more toned. John already wanted to lose weight, so he was not a problem. Tom and Thomas were the two that she would need to convince. Both were carrying too much weight for them to be healthy. She wanted her men to be healthy and live for a long time.

They all generally talked about Roy's upcoming birthday. He would be twenty-three on the seventh of November. Funnily, he was exactly six months older than Kay. She had just turned twenty-two on May seventh. They knew that Thomas would be home by then. They hoped that he would agree to go out to Roy's favorite steakhouse for his birthday celebration. He should be able to eat something healthy at the steakhouse.

Eleven

Roy spent as much time as he could in the evenings with Kay. His father was home again and had been so happy for Roy and Kay. He was subdued these days and very thankful that he had been given another chance to live. He surprisingly agreed to all of Selma's menus for their meals.

His doctors told him sternly that he needed to drop thirty to forty pounds and start a healthy cardio exercise program. He talked quietly with Roy one evening about joining the health club. He wanted Roy to be there to show him how everything worked.

The biggest change in Thomas, though, was when he started talking more openly to his wife about his feelings. Selma was happier than she had been in a very long time. She loved the fact that Thomas was starting to talk with her about whatever was bothering him.

She was kind and loving, and Thomas wondered why he had never confided in her before. His doctors told him not to keep things bottled up. It did his heart no good to be quietly frustrated or angry all the time.

Tom Junior watched the slow quiet changes in his father. He knew that he would benefit from working out, eating better, and opening up to people, too. He didn't want to end up like his dad, with a massive heart attack. Tom was a young man—only twenty-five. He could make his life a lot better if he could just change a few things.

His quiet call to Roy one night started him on the right path. Roy was so supportive and caring. Tom humbly asked Roy for his help. He wanted to dress nicer, lose some weight, and eat better. He saw how much John was changing and how much happier he was. Roy was so happy that his family was growing and changing.

When the family met at the steakhouse for Roy's birthday celebration, Roy looked at his mom with love. She was glowing with happiness. He was intrigued and pulled her a little to the side to talk with her for a moment.

"Mom, you look so pretty, tonight. I know how happy you are that Dad is back home, but there's something else, isn't there? You look like you have an inner glow. What's happened to make you so happy?" Roy held her hand and looked at his mom intently.

Selma smiled and said quietly, "Roy, your father has finally started to talk openly with me. We talk about his feelings—and mine. He wants us to be closer. He has apologized several times for being so unavailable to me for twenty years. This heart attack has changed him. He is more conscious of how we all feel about things. Yesterday, he and John talked for half an hour about dating. Can you imagine that? Thomas talking about dating with anyone!? He didn't even talk with me about it while we were dating all those years ago. It's like he is a new person. I feel so happy about that. I can finally talk with all my family. Even Tom started to come out of his shell and talk to me. John told me that Tom has talked with him recently, too. This heart attack really shocked us, but it has helped our family grow closer together."

Roy nodded and agreed. He had more talks lately with Tom and his dad than he previously had in his whole life. He was so happy for his mom. He had known for years how much she longed to be able to really talk with Thomas. Now, it seemed, they finally were. Roy hugged his mom tightly and told her how happy he was to hear all of that. His life was almost perfect right now.

Roy looked over to where Kay was sitting, gently flirting with her soon-to-be father-in-law. Thomas was chuckling softly, and his nice blue eyes twinkled. He very much admired and enjoyed Kay. Roy thought that his life would be perfect the day he and Kay got married.

As they were waiting to be seated at the restaurant, Roy looked at John and his sweet little date. This must be Caroline. John had described her perfectly. She was a slim young lady with long silky corn-colored hair that flowed over her small shoulders. Her hair looked to be too heavy for her slender neck. She was dressed in an ice blue dress that flatteringly showed off her small waist and pretty legs. He could see her excited blue eyes through her round wire-rimmed glasses.

While Roy watched them, he saw John gently take Caroline's small hand and help her to her seat. Roy approved of John's gentlemanly manners toward her. John treated Caroline as if she was someone very precious. Roy took notice of John's manner and was struck by how much he and his brother were like their father.

John introduced Caroline to everyone. "Mom and Dad, this is Caroline Humphries. She said that this steakhouse was her favorite one in Litton." Then he looked at Tom, Roy, and Kay, and introduced Caroline to them, as well. Roy could tell that John was very happy to have Caroline there as his date. John treated Caroline with gentleness and respect. Caroline's sweet face registered how happy she was to be on this date with him.

Kay sat on the other side of Caroline and asked her about school and her interests. She put Caroline at ease with meeting John's family on their first date. Kay silently applauded John for his gumption to have his first date with Caroline at a family event. He must know that everyone would be watching them.

She thought that John looked apprehensive but also proud. She planned to tell him later that she liked his new clothes. He had lost at least fifteen pounds and was looking much more fit than when she met him at Roy's apartment that day.

Kay was so proud of Roy for the active part that he was taking to ensure that his family became more fit. She saw that Tom and Thomas Senior had started to lose a little bit of weight and began to tone their muscles. Roy loved his family and just wanted everyone to be healthier. Because of his help, they were all becoming more fit.

Kay was happy that after Roy's birthday meal they decided to go to a club to dance. She adored dancing. She had never asked Roy if he liked to dance. He looked at her with a happy smirk on his face. He had taken ballroom dancing in college and had fallen in love with dancing closely with a partner.

For being a shy young man, he had made the most of dancing with the other members of his class. He was very light on his feet for being such a tall and lean man. Roy was very much looking forward to dancing with his beautiful Kay.

He looked at Kay and formally, but warmly, asked her, "May I have this dance, my dear?"

Kay beamed at him and said, "I thought you would never ask. I love dancing. I didn't know if you liked it, too."

"I'll love it even more with your beautiful person in my arms. I can't wait to slow dance with you, my love," he whispered softly into her ear.

Kay softly laughed and went into his arms. The band was playing a romantic song. Roy's eyes gleamed with happiness as he led Kay around the room in a beautiful dance.

John looked at Caroline and quietly asked her if she wanted to dance. She nodded her head. He gently took her hand and watched exactly how Roy danced. While John couldn't compete with Roy's finesse, he danced pretty well for a seventeen-year-old young man. He was pleased and surprised that Caroline followed his lead very well. She was so much smaller than he was. He felt like he was dancing with a thistledown.

Tom watched as his parents slowly circled the floor in a sweet dance. He hadn't known that his father could dance. Thomas Senior had never given any indication that he liked to, or even could, dance.

Tom sat there and thought about his family. His parents had started behaving like a devoted couple. It had taken his father's heart attack to get Thomas out of the rut that he had been in. He was finally now re-connecting with his wife. Roy and Kay were so in love and made Tom long for a relationship with a special woman, too. Even young John had started to date.

Tom had immediately liked Caroline. She was so perfect for John. He knew that John would likely meet other girls before he decided to settle down, but you never knew. Look at Roy—he had loved Kay since he was a junior in high school. Now they were getting married. Maybe Caroline was the one girl in the world for John.

Tom had so little chance to meet young women. He wasn't averse to taking a girl out. He was shy, but if he found the right girl, he could be every bit as romantic as Roy and John were. He watched his family have a wonderful time dancing and felt very lonely.

Kay looked around while she was dancing in Roy's arms. They felt extremely right around her. She saw Tom's wistful face as the song was coming to an end. Her hand tightened around Roy's. He looked at her face and saw compassion there.

"Darling Kay, what are you thinking about? You don't look like you are bowled over by my dancing. Do you want to stop?" Roy's voice was playful, but his eyes were intent. He was ever sensitive to Kay's feelings.

Kay smiled at Roy's slight teasing. "Roy, I was just looking at Tom's face when we danced past him. He looks lonely. Would you mind if I danced once with him?"

Roy's arms tightened around Kay a little tighter. How he loved this beautiful, generous, and caring woman. "Of course, I don't mind. It is sweet of you to care about Tom's feelings. I'll bet that he would love to dance once with you. But remember, you can also dance one time with Dad and one time with John, but all the rest of the dances are mine, okay?"

Kay smiled widely and said, "Yes, sir. Whatever you say, sir."

Roy smiled and nodded. He loved it when Kay was the tiniest bit sassy. He would dance with Caroline or his mom while Kay danced the next dance with Tom. He led the way over to where Tom was sitting. His parents had just taken their seats next to him. He imagined that his dad wanted to sit the next dance out. Thomas still tired quickly after his heart attack.

Kay very sweetly asked Tom to dance. She held out her hand to him and wouldn't take no for an answer. Roy asked his mom to dance. He flashed a quick grin at his father before taking his mom's hand and leading her out to the dance floor. Selma was surprised and pleased to see what a good dancer Roy was. He quietly told her that he had taken ballroom dancing classes in college.

They circled the room and talked quietly about their wonderful evening. Roy grinned at Kay and Tom when they passed him. Tom looked happy to be dancing with Kay. Roy watched them for a moment. Kay really was the loveliest woman that he had ever met. He was just so humbled that she had chosen to marry him out of all the men in the world. He was so very lucky.

Roy looked at John and Caroline when they passed him. John seemed very happy. Caroline had a happy smile on her face, too. Roy approved of John's new look. He had gotten his hair cut fashionably short and was wearing some snazzy new clothes. He looked good, now that he had dropped some weight and added some lean muscle to his upper body. Roy was proud of John for taking his health and exercise program so seriously.

Roy went on to dance once with Caroline. Kay sat out the next dance so she could converse with her future father-in-law, but after that, she asked John to dance. She complimented him on his new look. She told him that Caroline seemed to be such a sweet young lady. John nodded and emphatically agreed with her.

After dancing a slow dance with Thomas Senior, Kay gave herself up to the pleasure of dancing with Roy for the remainder of the evening. They danced so well together. She wondered if he would agree to them taking another ballroom dance class together. She wanted to learn how to dance the tango with him. She thought that it was such a romantic-looking dance.

Roy nuzzled her neck and held her tightly in his arms. He wanted to take her away and kiss her long and lingeringly, away from his family's smiling faces. Kay smelled so sweet, and she looked very beautiful. He trembled with his deep feelings for her. Kay looked up at him inquiringly. Roy just shook his head slightly and reached down to give Kay's perfect lips a feather-soft kiss. She smiled sweetly and kissed him back, just as softly. They floated around the room, oblivious of the rest of the world. It was like they were in their own private paradise.

John watched Roy and Kay. Roy knew all the moves. He certainly had Kay's obvious happy attention. John wondered if he dared to kiss Caroline when he took her home tonight. He had picked her up in the truck because his parents and Tom had come in the car. John had secretly practiced kissing the back of his hand, so he knew how much pressure to put on Caroline's lips. He didn't want to be too forceful with her. He just wanted to kiss her sweet pink lips gently for the first time. If she enjoyed it, then he would kiss her a little more firmly. His palms were sweaty just thinking about it.

Twelve

The wedding date was set for December 15th. They were going to have quite a small wedding with about twenty guests. Their wedding was going to be only immediate family and a few very close friends. After the wedding ceremony, they were all going to a nice hotel to have an elegant supper, with some dancing later. It was the kind of wedding that Kay wanted, so her parents had to go along with it. Roy was happy that Kay was happy. He didn't mind what kind of wedding they had—he was just excited to be getting married to her.

Kay's parents also wanted to have a big party for Kay and Roy so that all their extended family and friends could celebrate, too. Sterling had a great number of friends and business associates who wanted to help Anna and him celebrate their daughter's wedding. Kay and Roy went along with it, simply because it meant so much to Sterling and Anna.

Kay laughingly joked that they would likely receive every possible appliance for the kitchen and enough towels and sheets to last them half a lifetime. They didn't even need anything. Between his apartment and her furnished house, they had everything they needed for the home.

This huge party was to be on the day before their wedding. The biggest banquet hall in Litton was chosen as the location. Anna and Sterling had to convince Kay that she would enjoy it. It was her parents' way of giving her some of those trimmings that they felt that she was missing with a small quiet wedding.

Much to Kay's disappointment, her mother's wedding dress was too short for her. Anna had been a slim young bride, but she was five inches shorter than her daughter. Anna had a summer wedding, and her beautiful dress had been custom-made for her. While Kay was slender, she was also tall. She topped out at five feet eleven inches tall. Anna and Kay looked around Litton for the perfect wedding dress, but the town was too small to have enough selection.

Anna took Kay back to Chicago to look for her dress. They found one that turned Kay into a beautiful winter fairy. It was pure white silk, with sequins, pearls, and intricate lace on the lovely tight-fitting bodice. It made Kay's slender waist look so tiny. The long sleeves were lacy and had small pearl buttons along it from her wrist halfway up to her elbow. She would have to wear a very full slip underneath to make the skirt billow out. There was a long lacy train—running ten feet beyond the hem of the dress. Anna's beautiful lace veil looked lovely with the dress; Kay was happy that she would at least get to wear her mother's veil for the wedding.

Kay's Nana had given her a pair of beautiful diamond earrings when she graduated from college, and she wanted to wear them with her wedding dress. Because Roy was five inches taller than Kay, she was happy that she could wear the sweet lacy two-inch heels that she found to go with the dress. The whole ensemble made Kay look so beautiful.

Anna teared up when she saw her darling Kay wearing all her wedding clothes. Since it would be very cold in December, Anna and Sterling bought Kay a pure white fur coat. It was the most luxurious thing that Kay had ever worn. She thanked her parents and hugged and kissed them with love. They had been so generous to her for her whole life. Sterling gruffly told her that it was a parents' prerogative to give their daughter nice things. Roy would have the right to do that in the future, he told her.

Kay stayed in Chicago a few days, catching up with her friends and her uncle's family. She met up with Martie, who she asked to be her Maid of Honor. Martie had been genuinely surprised, but very happy for Kay and Roy. Kay explained that she was the girl that Roy had spoken to Martie about.

Martie shook her head and laughed. She had been holding off on talking to Kay about Roy ever since the opening day of the play. Martie thought that Roy liked Letty. Roy and Martie hadn't talked on the telephone for such a long time—mostly because of all the things that happened to him recently.

Roy quickly wrote to her and told her about his father's heart attack and that he would talk with her more, later. But after that, he got engaged and had been there to help his family get everything ready for Thomas' return home. Then there had been all the evenings at the health center helping John, and then his whole family learning how to exercise and tone their bodies. He squeezed in time to spend with his lovely fiancée, as well.

So, Martie had to hear their news from Kay. She said that she was delighted to be Kay's Maid of Honor. She would be paired with Tom, who was to be Roy's Best Man. John was going to be an usher at the wedding. Roy asked Kay if she still wanted to have a bunch of bridesmaids, but she said that she only wanted to have one, and that was Martie.

She asked Debbie to be her personal attendant and help her get dressed, among other things. Debbie agreed and said that she would like to see how everything went so that she could do the same for her own wedding next May. She hoped that there would be no issues for Kay's wedding. Kay had calmly told her that nothing was going to go wrong and that her wedding day would be perfect.

Since Kay didn't want to wear her wedding dress to the big party the day before the wedding, she decided to buy another white dress. She wanted to look bridal, but it should be something that she could wear again after the wedding. She found a beautiful tea-length gown in soft white chiffon. It was one of those beautiful flowing dresses that she had always seen the dancers wearing on the Lawrence Welk show. Kay and her Nana had watched that show for years, looking mostly at the dancers and their lovely dresses.

Because Kay had been a dancer for so many years, she liked to keep up with the new dances, especially the ballroom dances. She loved the pretty clothes that the beautiful women on the show wore. When she found that chiffon dress, she wished that her Nana could see her wear it. She hoped that somehow, Nana could see her from heaven tonight and on her wedding day.

Kay usually left her long hair loose, but she now experimented with putting it up in an elegant chignon. Anna told her that she had a lovely long neck and that a hairdo like that would show off her smooth skin and long lovely lines. She tried it with her wedding dress, diamond earrings, and veil, and found that her mom was right. She looked very elegant. Kay decided to wear her hair like that for both the party and her wedding day.

She hadn't shown that hairdo to Roy yet, and she hoped that he would like it. Roy had often quietly told her that her hair was so beautiful. He sometimes stroked her head and softly ran his hand down her long hair. He told her that he hoped she would keep it like that for as long as she could. Then he sometimes quoted her something romantic about long flowing beautiful raven hair.

Kay was so touched when he told her about what her hair looked like in high school. He told her that when she sat back in her seat in front of him, her hair often fell onto his desk. In the beginning, he had gently brushed it aside, but later, when his crush was deeper, he let it lay there on his desk. He had always been so tempted to touch it, but he hadn't dared to do that.

When he described it as a dark silken river, she just turned and looked at him with a shake of her head and a look of amazement on her face. Roy had to be the most romantic person that she had ever met. She couldn't believe that she hadn't seen how special and amazing he was, even back in high school. She kissed him long and tenderly for that confession of his.

Kay dressed carefully for the big party. She was a bit nervous. Her parents had invited half the town, it seemed. Kay was a social girl and liked parties as a rule, but she didn't really want to be the center of so much attention. Her hair went up beautifully, and her dress was gorgeous on her. She wore her Nana's earrings and her white fur coat. With her long slender dancer's legs, she looked like a dancer herself. She was pleased with her appearance.

Martie, who was staying with her until the wedding, told her that she literally looked like a million bucks. Martie was dressed up in a beautiful red lace dress with her new black patent leather two-inch heels. *She is very attractive,* Kay thought. They carefully hugged each other, so as not to disarrange their elegant hair and then set out for the party. Roy had gone to his parents' home and would be escorting them to the party. They would meet in the entryway.

Martie hadn't met her counterpart yet. She jokingly kept saying that this Hillman man might be just the right one for her. Kay laughingly told her that Tom was a sweetie, but he was even more quiet than Roy was. Martie said, "That's okay, I like a challenge."

Kay and Martie got there a little early. No one was around yet. They had even beat her parents there. Since Martie was staying with Kay for a few days, and Debbie was still living there, Sterling and Anna were staying in the hotel where the wedding dinner would be tomorrow. It was a small, but very luxurious hotel, which was just right for her parents. They liked luxury, but it should not be ostentatious.

Debbie was currently at her fiancé's house, but she and Donny would come to the party a little later. Debbie would be staying at Kay's house while they were on their honeymoon but would move out the day before Roy and Kay got back. She would temporarily be going back to her parents' home until February when she would room with another good friend until her May wedding to Donny.

She jokingly claimed that she would become a good packer since she had to do it so often. No, she was okay with moving back to her parents' home for a few months. Her mom wanted to be there to help her with any last-minute things before her wedding.

Roy, his parents, and Tom got there at the same time as Kay's parents. John had the truck and was bringing Caroline to the party. They would be arriving a little later because Caroline had another event to go to before she could come to this party.

After hugs all around, Roy took Kay's hand and walked her around the banquet center. It was beautifully decorated in red and white. There were flowers everywhere. Anna planned everything and had made it into the beautiful oasis that it was. Roy squeezed

Kay's hand as they walked around. He snuck in a few sweet kisses, too.

"My beautiful Kay, you look like a bride today. I know that this isn't your wedding dress, but it could be. You look amazing. I really like your hair like that. You almost look too perfect to be kissed. I don't want to smudge anything." Roy's tone worshiped her.

"You better not hold back your kisses, mister! If you do, I'll just have to kiss you first. Let's see you do something about that," Kay's tone was playful and flirtatious.

Roy laughed with appreciation. He loved Kay's sassy and impish side. He could never pull off talking like that himself, but he thought that Kay was so endearing when she was sassy like that. He couldn't get enough of her. He just had one more day to get through—and then she would be his wife, forever. Just the thought of that put a lovely smile on his face.

"Why do you look like that, Roy? You look so ecstatic. What are you thinking about?" Kay wanted to share Roy's happy thoughts.

Roy was so grateful to his mom for showing him how to share his feelings with someone. He wanted to always be able to talk with Kay and share his most intimate feelings with her. He already knew that she loved his romantic side. When he quoted a poem to her, or just spoke directly from his heart, she listened quietly to him and then usually hugged and kissed him and thanked him for sharing with her and for just being Roy.

Roy flushed a little and looked lovingly into her eyes. "I was just thinking that tomorrow you would finally be my wife, forever."

Roy was not disappointed. Kay looked like she wanted to cry for a second, but she didn't. Instead, she hugged and kissed him and said, "Roy, I'm so happy that I could cry. I'm looking forward to tomorrow, too. I want you to be my husband forever, too. Thank you for those wonderful words, darling."

Martie came up to them and teased them about kissing all the time. Roy protested lightly and said that this was the first time that he had seen Kay today. He was just getting his daily quota of kisses in before the hordes of guests arrived. Martie had to agree with that. She grinned at Roy. He had certainly come out of his shell since that night of the play.

Kay smiled at the two of them. She enjoyed seeing Roy banter with Martie. He never did it with her. He was always so loving and romantic with her. She was going to have to encourage some banter with him after they were married. She thought that Roy was just so afraid of hurting her feelings, that he hardly ever joked around with her.

"So how come no one has introduced me to that brother of yours, Roy? I want to see if he is Mr. Right for me." Martie joked with them.

"Mr. Right, huh? Somehow, I don't think that you two will find much in common. But you never know, opposites attract sometimes, don't they?" Roy smirked at Martie.

Kay laughed outright. The three friends walked around, looking for Tom. They found him in a quiet corner, talking with his father. They both looked up when Roy said Tom's name.

"Tom, I want to introduce you to Martie. She's Kay's Maid of Honor. You'll be walking down the aisle with her tomorrow." Roy smiled at his older brother with a broad smile. Tom looked at Martie with so much admiration. Roy didn't blame him. Martie really did look very pretty, tonight.

"Martie, this is my brother, Tom. He's a decent fellow. I think that you guys will get along just fine. By the way, he does know how to dance, so he probably won't step on your toes when you dance tomorrow." Roy's eyes were dancing with fun.

Martie shot Roy a quick glance that seemed to say, *Hey, let me make my own first impressions, okay, buddy?*

She smiled nicely at Tom and said, "It's nice to meet you, Tom. I hope that Roy is right and that you won't step on me when we dance. I'll try not to do that, too. I can dance, but I'm certainly not Ginger Rogers." Her eyes twinkled up at Tom.

He was a good five inches taller than she was. He was five feet eleven inches tall, while she was just shy of five feet six inches. Martie liked a taller man, especially as a dance partner. Taller men made her feel more petite and feminine. That's something that she secretly liked but would never have admitted to anyone.

Tom stood up and gently took Martie's hand. His quiet hello had her smiling. *Tom really is as quiet as Roy had been,* Martie thought. Roy had finally opened up. Maybe she could get Tom to do that, too. She only had tonight and tomorrow to work on him, though. Oh well, she might as well start now. She linked her arm with his and pulled him along with her. They walked around the banquet hall looking at all the decorations.

Thomas looked at Roy and Kay and chuckled. "It looks like poor Tom is going to be forced to respond to that young lady. She's a pretty girl, and I think a very outgoing one, too. I wonder how Tom will deal with that." He laughed again.

Roy and Kay just grinned back at him. "Tom's a big boy, Dad. I think that Martie is the perfect person to help Tom have a great time at our wedding. He probably doesn't know what hit him. If I know Martie, she'll have him out on the dance floor doing the tango or something. By the way, Tom does know how to dance, doesn't he, Dad? I just said that to Martie. I really don't know if he does know how to dance."

Thomas laughed loudly and said in an amused voice, "Somehow, I don't think it will even matter if he can dance. That Martie will probably lead, anyway."

They all chuckled about that for a few minutes. Then Thomas looked at Kay and said softly, "My goodness, Kay, you sure are a beautiful girl. Roy must be so proud to be your fiancé. I'm so happy to finally have a daughter. You are exactly the one that I would have chosen." Then he bent over and gently kissed her cheek.

Kay was overcome. "Mr. Hillman, thank you for those beautiful words. Now I know where Roy gets his romantic side. I would be proud to be your daughter." She kissed Thomas' cheek back.

He put one arm gently around her shoulder and said quietly, "In that case, would you call me Thomas? And I know that Selma would love it if you would call her by her name."

Kay looked quickly at Roy. He smiled at her. He was shocked by the words that had just come out of his father's mouth. He had never in his life thought of his father as being a romantic man, but now he wasn't so sure. Maybe his father really did have a romantic soul, and no one ever knew it. *Well, maybe Mom did*, he thought.

Kay gently squeezed Thomas' hand and said, "Thank you, Thomas. I'm so happy that you think of me as a daughter. I will think of you as my second dad, now. And I would be happy to call Mrs. Hillman Selma if she would really like that."

Roy walked Kay and his father around until they found Selma. She was wearing a new dress tonight, and Roy thought that she looked pretty in it. Thomas must have thought so, too, because he kissed

Selma's cheek and looked at her with love. That was the first time that Roy had ever seen his dad do that. *Well, well, things are just getting better and better for Mom,* Roy thought happily.

"Honey, I've just been talking with Kay. She has agreed to call me Thomas and you Selma. What do you think about that?" Thomas quietly asked his wife.

Selma smiled and turned to look at Kay. She said, "Oh, Kay, you look so lovely. Thank you. I would love it if you called me Selma. I have always wanted a daughter, and you are so sweet and kind. You're exactly who I would have chosen if God would have blessed me with my own daughter." She leaned forward and kissed Kay's cheek.

Kay looked at her with affection and said, "Thank you so much, Selma. I will think of you as my second mother. Roy always talks about you with much love. I'm so happy that we will be family after tomorrow."

The four of them talked quietly for a few more minutes until Anna and Sterling hurriedly came up to them. They quickly smiled at Thomas and Selma before Anna said, "Kay, darling, you and Roy need to be just inside the door to receive your guests. They will all be starting to arrive in less than ten minutes. We'd like you to greet everyone as they come in. Dad and I will introduce you to anyone that you don't know."

She looked at Selma and Thomas and said with a gentle smile, "Mr. and Mrs. Hillman, please come, too, if you would like. Sterling and I would be happy to introduce you to everyone as they come in."

Thomas thanked her but quietly said that he wanted to just have a seat and relax. He was getting tired from all the standing around. Everyone there knew that he was still recovering from his heart attack.

Anna nodded and patted his arm gently as she said, "Okay, but please let me know if you want to meet anyone, or if you need anything. There is a comfortable side room that goes with the banquet hall. There are a few couches and armchairs in there if you feel like you want to get away from this crowd. I'm only telling the members of the wedding party about it. This party might get quite loud, so please use it whenever you feel like getting away. I'm sure that this party will go on for three or four hours. It's that door over there that has the 'Do Not Enter' sign on it. Please just disregard the sign and go in whenever you want. There is a fridge in there with bottled water and soft drinks in it, too. Help yourself. Well, have a wonderful time."

She looked at Kay and said, "Are you ready, darling? Grab Roy and let's go, okay?"

Kay and Roy walked away with them. Now the party was about to begin. Roy held Kay's hand as they walked. She was just so beautiful that he couldn't stop looking at her. He gently caressed her wrist as they walked. Kay's hand squeeze and sweet smile at him told him that she liked his hand caresses.

Roy and Kay welcomed John and Caroline when they came in. Caroline was gently pretty in a pale green velvet dress. It was a perfect foil for her long pretty, blonde hair.

"Caroline, you look so pretty. I'm so glad that you could make it to the party. I know that you had another event to go to tonight," Kay said quietly to her. Caroline's shy smile was very attractive.

"Thank you, Kay. You look so beautiful. I'm glad that I was able to come to your party," she said. Caroline turned to look at Roy and said, "Roy, you look very handsome, too. I hope that you have a lovely evening. We'll see you later, okay?" With that she looked at

John and took his arm to lead them away. There were many people waiting in line behind them. She knew better than to hold up a reception line. There would be plenty of time to talk with John's family as the night progressed.

John and Caroline easily found his parents. They sat and chatted for half an hour. Thomas said that he wanted to check out that quiet side room. He pulled Selma to her feet. The four of them walked into the quiet room. It was a comfortable room with several sets of couches and armchairs. John saw the fridge and got all of them a cold bottle of water. They chatted a few more minutes in peace until John said that he wanted to show Caroline around the banquet hall.

John was already planning to bring Caroline back here sometime this evening, hopefully when no one else was around. He wanted some private time with her. They had been going out together for five weeks, and he wanted to kiss her in private. He thought back to their first kiss. He had been shy about it, but he discovered that Caroline was shy, too. That first little peck on her lips had progressed recently into much more satisfying kissing.

Caroline had been surprised at first when John kissed her with some expertise. She didn't know about his practice kissing the back of his hand. She liked John, and she liked kissing him, too. He was the first young man that she had ever dated, so kissing was as new to her as it was to him. He was very charming and sweet to her. He treated her like she was special. She really liked that about him. He had also quietly stuck up for some kids at school who didn't do that for themselves. In her eyes, John Hillman was a very nice and attractive young man.

They walked around until they ran into Martie and Tom. Tom smiled at Caroline and then introduced them to Martie.

"Martie, this is my kid brother, John, and his date, Caroline. John and Caroline are seniors in high school."

Martie looked surprised and said, "I didn't know that Roy had another brother. Are there any more Hillman children lurking around that I don't know about?" she asked with a wide smile.

"No, it's just us three men," said Tom with a grin. This Martie sure had a fun sense of humor. He just couldn't get used to the idea of a woman that pretty being so forward. She had been surprising him all evening. He found that he kind of liked the way she took charge and then did what she said she would do. He was a shy man, and never thought about just doing the things that he thought quietly about. He could learn a lot from Martie.

Anna had been right—the party was long and loud. Everyone seemed to be having a lot of fun, though. Roy saw Tom and Martie a few times. Poor Tom had a bemused look on his face. Martie had a happy look on her face. *She is probably loving pushing Tom around,* Roy thought.

He thought that she was born to be a bossy mother or a teacher. He knew that she was a nurse, but he couldn't imagine what her bedside manner would be like. He could just hear her saying to a patient, "Now listen up. You're going to get better, or else!"

He chuckled to himself when he thought that. Kay wanted to know what was so amusing, so he had to tell her. She laughed out loud. *It's so great when Roy comes up with something so funny,* she thought. He certainly knew Martie. Kay thought the same thing about Martie sometimes.

There was a very long table set up to receive the wedding gifts that people brought. It was soon overflowing, and the banquet manager had to bring in another table to accommodate the surplus of gifts. It looked like there were hundreds of them to Roy. *Oh, for goodness' sake,* he thought, *what are we going to do with all of them?* They really didn't need anything.

Anna had decided that it would take too much time if Kay and Roy opened their wedding gifts at the party. She had asked everyone to write down their names and addresses in the guest book so that Kay and Roy could send them a thank you card for their presence tonight and their gift.

Sterling and Anna would make sure that the gifts all got safely back to Kay's house. That's where the wedding gifts from tomorrow would go as well. Roy and Kay planned to have the wedding party and parents over to watch them open the gifts when they came back from their honeymoon.

Roy had never been out of the United States before, and it had been a few years since Kay had gone to Europe with her parents. Since they both spoke fluent French, they had decided to go to France and tour the country for two weeks. They had the best time planning their route and accommodations. Christmas in France would be exciting, too.

It was a very big surprise when both sets of parents told them that their trip was their wedding gift to the couple. Roy and Kay had protested and said that it was much too much, but both sets of parents had shaken their heads. They really wanted to pay for the trip.

Roy's mom confided to him that Sterling and Anna had been so sweet about it. They offered to pay for the entire trip and say that it was from both sets of parents. They reminded the Hillmans that they had just had a lot of medical expenses to pay for.

However, Thomas quietly told them that he and Selma had a special account at the bank that they kept just for their boys' future weddings. Sterling asked Thomas candidly how much he could afford, and Thomas had been upfront and told him. Sterling thanked the Hillmans and said that they could write a check to him for whatever amount they wanted. The trip would be equally from both sets of parents. Thomas and Selma were pleased and surprised at their generosity.

It seems as if the quiet room should be renamed the "Kissing Room". During the evening, Roy and Kay, John and Caroline, Thomas and Selma, and even Tom and Martie found time to smooch a little as they sat on the couches, away from the rest of the party.

Martie asked Tom if they could sit quietly for a few minutes. He was weary from the crowd by then and readily agreed. They sat on the couch with their cold water. Tom sat a little bit away from her. He didn't want to seem forward or scare her. Martie, however, had no problem with scooching over right next to him. She laid her hand on his arm and smiled warmly at his face. He trembled a little bit. He wasn't accustomed to spending so much time with a pretty girl.

Martie could see how shy Tom was. She wanted to kiss him, so she did. She just leaned over and kissed Tom right on the mouth. She was happy when his arm slowly came around her shoulders, and he pulled her closer to deepen their kiss. It was very pleasant. She looked up at his face and saw that his eyes were closed.

Tom was shocked and surprised for just a minute when Martie initiated the kiss. However, he liked it and wanted to deepen the kiss. He was surprised that he was kissing a woman he just met an hour or two ago. He had never been confident enough to do that before. Since Martie started the kiss, she must like him a little. He certainly enjoyed her company. He closed his eyes and gave himself up to that kiss.

When the kiss ended, they pulled apart and looked at each other. Martie's cheeks were pink, and she boldly said, "I'm the kind of person who is up front with people. I say what I am thinking and do what I want to do, as far as possible. I wanted to kiss you, Tom, so I did. I hope you don't mind. It seemed as if you enjoyed it, too."

Tom smiled shyly at her and nodded. He said, "Martie, I didn't mind that you kissed me. I did enjoy it, too. You certainly broke the ice. I might not have been confident enough to kiss you at all in the short time that we will spend together. Thank you. It was a great kiss." With that, he stopped and blushed bright red.

The door opened just then, and Roy and Kay came in. They saw how close Tom and Martie were sitting to each other and noted the flushes on their cheeks. They both smiled when they thought that Martie probably kissed Tom. Both knew Tom, and they were sure that he would not have initiated a kiss with Martie. They sat on the other couch talking to Martie and Tom about the party.

Martie saw Roy take Kay's hand and gently caress her wrist. She knew that Roy was probably longing to kiss Kay away from all the guests. She pulled Tom up and jokingly said, "Come on, Fred, let's start the dancing. Your brother promised that you wouldn't trod all over my toes. I spoke to the band before I met you, and they said they would play whatever anyone wanted to hear. They said that people could also dance, if they wanted to."

She looked quickly at Roy and winked at him as she said, "See you later, my friends. Enjoy a nice respite from the crowds."

Roy grinned at her. He knew that Martie knew that he was longing to give his Kay a long and tender kiss. After they left, Kay opened her mouth to say something, but he quickly swept her into his arms and kissed her lingeringly. By the end of the kiss, Kay had forgotten what she was about to say to him. They both felt better after that kiss. It was a little difficult to be reminded every minute that they were to marry tomorrow. Their kiss just now took away some of the pressure they had been feeling.

As they sat quietly holding hands, Roy's parents came in. They had a nice little chat before saying that they should go back to the party. Thomas looked tired and uncomfortable. Selma got them some water and sat down next to him. She put her hand on his arm and gently stroked it. He turned and smiled wearily at her.

Roy and Kay smiled at them as they left. Outside the door, Kay asked Roy, "Do you think that your dad is okay, Roy? He looked really tired and even kind of ill."

Roy nodded and said, "I know, I saw that, too. Earlier, I made my mom promise that she would come and get me if Dad seemed too tired or ill. She knows the signs to look for in a heart attack. She was worried that this party would be too much for him. She'll come and find me if she thinks that something is wrong. I'm hoping that it is just tiredness. They are smart to sit out for a while every hour or so. They want to stay until the end of the party, so they might just spend the last hour or so in the quiet room. Thank you for the kiss, my darling. I just couldn't wait any more to kiss you." Roy's face was suddenly happy and smiling.

Kay squeezed his hand and said softly, "If your parents hadn't come in just then, I was about to kiss you again. But I guess that I'll have to be fine with that one wonderful kiss you gave me. Let's make the rounds and talk with as many people as possible. This party means a lot to my parents. I want to show them my appreciation for all they have done and given us, okay, dear?"

Roy squeezed her hand back and said, "Of course, darling. Just think, by this time tomorrow, we'll be man and wife. I am just so amazed and awed by that. My dearest hopes and dreams would have come true." With that, he bent and gently kissed her smooth satiny cheek. She smiled back at him, and they strolled away.

Roy was planning to spend the night at his parents' farm. His mom wanted to cherish him a little. It was the last night that she would have that privilege. After tomorrow, Kay would have the privilege of cherishing Roy.

He smiled at her when Selma brought it up with him but agreed to spend the night with them. Since they all had to get dressed up for the wedding, she wanted him to relax in bed until the other men were ready. Then he could put on his tuxedo.

Kay's parents decided to spend tonight at her house. Anna wanted to make sure that Kay had breakfast in bed and a leisurely time to get dressed. The wedding ceremony wasn't until eleven o'clock, since you could never depend on the Minnesota weather in December. Guests might have to shovel out their driveways or drive slowly if the roads were bad.

After he hugged and kissed Kay goodnight, much to the delight of their families, Roy went out to start his father's car. It was a cold night. Snowflakes were starting to fall on his dark hair. The weatherman predicted a few inches of snow overnight. Roy was glad that they would have extra time in the morning to shovel the drive and get to the church. Tom and John promised to shovel the drive, so that Thomas and Roy could get dressed at their leisure.

Sterling and Anna had to get things settled at the banquet hall before they left, so they said that they would get to Kay's house in an hour. Kay and Martie left in her Pontiac. The roads were just starting to get a little slippery. Kay hoped that her parents would drive safely. When she and Martie got home, they got into their pajamas and snuggled up in blankets while they waited for Anna and Sterling to get there.

Sterling arranged with the banquet hall to store all the gifts until he could get some help bringing them to Kay's house. Tom and John volunteered to meet him in two days to help him load up the presents and take them over to Kay's house.

Sterling and Anna arrived and commented on how typical it was that it would snow on an important day. Sterling hoped that the snow would not get too deep. That would make everything messy and frustrating for everyone. They were all thankful that the wedding was going to be a small one tomorrow.

If the snow fell all night, and the drifts got too deep by tomorrow morning, Sterling would have to call his friend in the snow plowing business to clear a path so that the wedding party could get to the church and the hotel.

Kay made sure that everything was ready for the morning. She and Roy would be coming back to her house tomorrow night to sleep. Their flight to France wouldn't be leaving until the following morning at nine am.

CHAPTER

Thirteen

When Roy woke up the next morning, he just lay in bed grinning. Today was his wedding day. He would marry the only woman he had ever loved. As lovely as Kay had been last night, he just knew that she would be even more beautiful today in her wedding gown. He heard his parents talking downstairs, so he got up. It was early—only six-thirty. He really didn't have to be up for hours yet.

As he walked down the stairs, he looked out of the window. He stared in amazement. There had to be at least a foot or more of new snow on the ground and the snow was still falling. He hurried down the stairs and into the kitchen. His mom and dad were talking quietly. They had seen the snow, too, and were wondering what they should do. They looked at Roy when he came in and sat down.

"Roy, you shouldn't be up, yet. You should be relaxing. You have a busy day ahead of you." His mom was quietly fussing over him.

Roy smiled at her and cheerfully said, "Well, what do you think of the weather? It's a fine way to start my wedding day, don't you think?"

His parents both looked at Roy quickly to see if he was upset. He didn't look upset, so they both relaxed.

"Don't worry, son. The weatherman says that the snow should stop in an hour or so. The boys will get the driveway shoveled out in plenty of time. The only thing that I'm worried about is the condition of the roads. I really hope that the snowplows will be out as soon as the snow stops to clear the roads. It's twenty miles to the church, and it will be tough on the car if the roads are not clear, although we could take the truck if we need to. It would mean a few trips, but that's okay. We'll just start a bit earlier." Thomas' voice was strong and confident. He didn't want Selma or Roy to worry about anything.

When he found out that Kay and Roy planned a December 15th wedding, Sterling had contacted his old buddy, Phil, a month ago and said that he might need his help on that day. Phil owned one of the larger snowplow businesses in town. You never knew what the weather was going to be like in Minnesota in December. Phil had given Sterling priority regarding using his snowplow for that day.

Sterling was up early and checking the weather channels. The snow was supposed to stop falling by 9:00 am. Even after the snow stopped falling, they still had to get through all the snow that was already on the roads.

Now Sterling called Phil and explained the situation. He had to get himself and the four women with him to the church for the wedding, and later, to the hotel. Luckily, it was only five miles to the church. He wanted to help the Hillmans, too. Thomas had said last night that their farm was twenty miles from the church. If Phil could plow the main road from the church to the Hillman farm, they would be able to drive their car and follow the plow back to the church. Sterling promised to pay for Phil's services for the entire day.

After Phil promised to help him, Sterling called Thomas Hillman at 8:00 am. He told him about the plan. Thomas was so grateful for his gracious offer of help. Thomas shared the plan with Selma and his boys. Then Selma made her family a wonderful breakfast, which they all ate with appetite.

Roy wanted to call Kay and reassure her that everything would be okay, but he wasn't sure if he should. Anna had jokingly told him last night that he couldn't see or talk with Kay on their wedding day until she walked down the aisle toward him on her father's arm. Would a reassuring phone call to his love count against him? He didn't want to upset anyone. He just wanted Kay to be free from stress and worry. He hoped that Sterling would reassure Kay that the whole Hillman family would arrive at the church as soon as the plow cleared the way to the church for them.

At 9:00 am, Tom and John went out to shovel a path from the garage to the road, so that when the plow got there, they would be able to follow it right away to the church. Roy had a lot of nervous energy, so he went out to help his brothers. They had a hilarious time throwing the fresh cold snow over each other. They hadn't played like that since they were kids.

Thomas and Selma stood hand-in-hand watching their boys from the window. Thomas squeezed Selma's hand gently, looked at her, and said, "Our boys, Selma. Aren't they a fine bunch?"

Selma nodded and smiled widely. She finally had the loving family that she had always wanted, and now one of her lambs was leaving them today. "Yes, Thomas, they sure are a good-looking bunch of young men. We did well." With that she leaned over and kissed his cheek. He just smiled nicely at her and squeezed her hand again.

Roy enjoyed his last day at his old home. His family was in high spirits, even with all the heavy snow that was still falling.

They all decided to wear older clothes and boots on the way to the church, just in case they got stuck in the snow. There were dressing rooms at the church that they could use once they safely got there.

The men all showered and shaved and put their tuxedos in plastic so any snow or wetness wouldn't ruin them. Selma was allowed to get completely dressed in her lovely "mother-of-the-groom" dress. With her makeup and lovely dress, Roy hardly recognized her. Still, he was both proud and humbled that his hardworking mom looked her very best for him. He wasn't the only Hillman male who had taken notice.

Thomas looked at her with admiration and love. Selma's face pinkened when she saw her husband of twenty-six years look at her that way. If they had trouble with the car, Selma would not need to do anything except sit tight in her seat while her men took care of everything.

*　*　*

Back at Kay's house, everything was calm. Sterling told everyone there the plan for the day. He told them that Phil would clear the road so that the Hillmans could get to the church in their car. Kay was so happy to hear that. She had been afraid that the snowstorm would cause them to put off or delay her wedding. Even though she and Roy only had a two-month engagement, she felt like she had been waiting for this day to come for such a long time. She definitely wanted to marry Roy today—even in a snowstorm.

The ladies decided to wait until they got to the church to change into their wedding finery. They didn't want to be dragging their long skirts through snow and slush. Anna made them all a lovely breakfast. Kay was too excited to eat much of it, though.

Phil arrived in front of Kay's house by 9:00 am. He had already cleared the route from Kay's house to the church so that Anna's Bentley Corniche could get there without any trouble. Sterling had planned to take them all to the church in a classic white limo, but it rode too low and might get stuck. Anna's Bentley had enough room for all of them and the suspension was higher. Sterling's racy sports car wouldn't be very good in all that snow—besides it was too small to hold all of them.

They piled all their things in the Bentley's roomy trunk and got in. There was plenty of time for them to get dressed at the church. Sterling took the wheel and followed Phil's snowplow the five miles to the church. His four passengers were silent, thinking of what they needed to do once they arrived at the church. The streets were slippery, but the Bentley maneuvered along them well.

Sterling dropped them off right in front of the church door and quietly told them to go in. He would bring in their things from the trunk. Phil helped him carry everything in. Once inside, Anna ushered all the ladies to the Bride's room so they could get dressed. Sterling thanked Phil and sent him off to plow the roads to the Hillman farm. Phil thought that he would be back with the Hillmans in roughly an hour.

Phil's snowplow arrived at the Hillman farm about 9:40 am. They all jumped into Thomas' car and followed the plow all the way to the church. When they saw all the snow that Phil had plowed to the side of the road, they knew that their car would never have made it to the church without Phil's help.

Thomas had his thank you speech to Sterling all set in his head. They arrived at the church at 10:30 am. There was still half an hour before the wedding, and Roy and his brothers and father knew that they would have plenty of time to get dressed. Tom rushed Roy to the Groom's dressing room so that he wouldn't accidentally see Kay before the wedding. Since Selma was already beautifully dressed, she went to the Bride's room to say hello to Kay and Anna.

Kay was so happy to see Selma and hear that the Hillmans had all made it to the church. Her darling Roy was just a few feet away, getting ready, too. Her face broke out in a lovely smile. Anna and Selma could read every expression on her face. The bad weather was not going to stop Kay from marrying the love of her life that morning.

Anna cried when she saw her darling Kay in her exquisite wedding dress and veil. She knew that she was biased, but she thought that her baby was the most beautiful bride that ever lived. Kay was a little pale, but so very elegant and lovely. She looked so happy, too.

Fourteen

The organist had arrived just in time to play two songs before she started "The Wedding March". None of the other guests had been able to get to the church, so only the family members were there. Neither Kay nor Roy minded the fact that only their families were there to see them wed. It was their day, after all.

Luckily, Anna and Selma had decorated the church yesterday, and it looked old and beautiful. The flowers smelled so fresh, and the flickering candles shed a soft glow over everyone. John had already ushered Selma, Thomas, and Anna into the front pews. Roy was standing near the altar, so proud and handsome, while he waited for his lovely Kay to walk toward him.

Martie and Debbie brought Kay into the foyer to meet up with her father. When Sterling saw his beautiful daughter, he felt tears come into his eyes. It was a sad day for him—giving away his sweet Kay. However, he knew that Roy was a fine man and that he would never have to worry about Kay's happiness again.

He was reminded of his own wedding day. Kay looked so much like his lovely Anna. He reached over and kissed Kay's soft cheek. Her luminous blue eyes looked up at him, and he saw his daughter's love for him. A big lump came into his throat when he saw that. He gently squeezed her hand and said, "You look so lovely, my dear. Your mother and I just want you to be happy. We love you so much."

Sterling gently took her arm and whispered "Ready?" when "The Wedding March" started. Kay just nodded; she was too emotional to speak.

Martie smiled at Tom as he took her arm inside the church. He was shocked at the way his heart pounded when he saw Martie. She was so lovely in her gorgeous red lace dress. She thought that he looked very handsome in his dark gray tuxedo with the red cummerbund. *Today might be kind of interesting*, she thought happily.

Roy's eyes sought out Kay's face the minute she started walking down the aisle with her father. Her beauty took his breath away. He loved her so much. Kay kept her eyes on Roy, too, as she and her father walked down the aisle. Then Sterling stopped right in front of him, kissed Kay's cheek, and offered her arm to Roy. He looked at Sterling and quietly said, "Thank you" before gently taking Kay's arm and walking her the short distance to the altar.

The wedding mass was lovely. They had written their own vows to each other. Silent tears came down Kay's lovely face at Roy's words of love to her. Her sweet vows to him made Roy tear up, too. Their families saw the tears and couldn't help their own eyes from tearing up. These two beautiful young people were just so much in love with each other. That made them all so happy.

As Roy and Kay walked out of the church, hand-in-hand, they both sighed deeply. They had made it! Roy's father was there, and the snowstorm had not stopped the wedding. They looked at each other and smiled deeply. Now that the nerve-racking part was over, they both wanted to enjoy the rest of the day.

While they waited in the foyer for their families to congratulate them, Roy looked intently at Kay. He anticipated that she would look incredibly lovely today, and he was right. He was almost too afraid to touch her; she was so exquisite. But then she grinned up at him and winked.

He felt a bubble of laughter at her playfulness. Just when he wanted to look at her and worship her with his eyes, she took away the seriousness of the moment and made him laugh. He was going to love being married to this amazingly beautiful, fun, sweet, kind, smart, and vivacious woman.

When the families had hugged, kissed, and congratulated them, the newly married couple went to the door and peeked out. The snow was still falling heavily, and the wind was starting to blow that snow around. Luckily, Phil was still around. He had sat in the back of the church and watched the wedding. Now he was back in his snowplow and clearing the church parking lot. He had cleared the streets that led from the church to the hotel earlier but had to do it again because so much new snow had fallen.

The two families gathered all their belongings and got back into their cars. The cars followed Phil's plow to the hotel. They were just glad to be able to leave the church.

The wedding reception at the hotel was very quiet, but nice. After eating a wonderfully delicious dinner, they walked a few steps over to the fireplace room, where they eased themselves into overstuffed chairs arranged around the largest fireplace any of them had ever seen. The fire crackled and flickered as they chatted in warm conviviality.

Before they could drift off to a nice midday nap, the hotel manager put on some romantic music, and they all arose to dance for a while. The only ones who didn't have a partner were John and Debbie, so they laughed together and danced a few times. Debbie's fiancé, Donny, was not able to get to the wedding. Caroline had come to the party the night before because she was not available to come to the wedding.

Martie and Tom danced many times with each other. Roy was amused to see that Tom painstakingly kept himself from stepping on Martie's feet, but he was no Fred Astaire. Nonetheless, Martie jokingly called him "Fred", and, in turn, Tom called her "Ginger". It appeared that they were having a wonderful time together.

Roy's ballroom dancing classes in college served him well. Since Kay had danced most of her life, she was a beautiful and graceful dancer. Even though the room was small and cozy, they floated around like they were on a professional dance floor. Everyone thought how beautiful they looked, dancing together.

That evening, Roy called the airport and found that all planes had been grounded and there would be no flights out until much later tomorrow after the snowstorm had stopped and the runways had been cleared. Since they couldn't get back to Kay's house, the hotel offered Roy and Kay the Honeymoon Suite for the night.

The hotel had enough rooms for everyone. Tom and John shared a room, and Martie and Debbie shared another one. Since everyone except Selma had gone to the church in other clothes and dressed in their wedding clothes once they got there, they had something to change into. They all stayed in their wedding clothes until they finished their supper. Then most of them went to their rooms and changed into their casual clothes for the rest of the night. Since Anna and Sterling had been staying there, Anna had some extra clothes that she could share with Selma.

The newlyweds were joined once again in the fireplace room by everyone else, where they talked and played board games provided for them by the hotel. Roy and Kay stayed in their wedding clothes the entire time. Roy loved the way his bride looked in her gorgeous wedding dress. He had not been able to take his eyes off her all day and evening.

Kay also thought that Roy was extremely handsome, and she was proud to be his wife. They sat, all cuddled up, on a loveseat in the room, not paying much attention to anyone else. They talked softly to each other and managed to get in a few great kisses. The others left them alone—they were, after all, newly married.

The wind howled and the snow fell all evening. No one cared, because they were all safe and comfortable in the luxurious little hotel.

It had been a long day, and people drifted off to their rooms a few at a time. When they finally walked up to their luxury suite, Roy unlocked the door and lifted his lovely wife over the threshold of their room. He gently set her down, and they smiled sweetly at each other. Roy finally whispered the sweet and romantic words that he had been waiting all day to say to her and pulled her tenderly into his arms. Now their life together could begin.

www.ingramcontent.com/pod-product-compliance
Lightning Source LLC
Chambersburg PA
CBHW051450050726
47593CB00005B/2009